THE SHEIKH'S FORBIDDEN LOVER

THE SHEIKHS OF HAVILAH
BOOK THREE

DIANA FRASER

The Sheikh's Forbidden Lover
by Diana Fraser

© 2020 Diana Fraser

She was bought once, he'll buy her again...

—The Sheikhs of Havilah—
The Sheikh's Secret Baby
Bought by the Sheikh
The Sheikh's Forbidden Lover
Surrender to the Sheikh
Taken for the Sheikh's Harem

—Desert Kings—
Wanted: A Wife for the Sheikh
The Sheikh's Bargain Bride
The Sheikh's Lost Lover
Awakened by the Sheikh
Claimed by the Sheikh
Wanted: A Baby by the Sheikh

—Secrets of the Sheikhs—
The Sheikh's Revenge by Seduction
The Sheikh's Secret Love Child
The Sheikh's Marriage Trap

https://www.dianafraser.com

PROLOGUE

*R*oshan entered the vast hall in the desert castle where the three kings of Havilah met each month to discuss their countries' affairs, and glanced around. He was instantly on edge. Something was wrong. He could sense it, and he could see it in how Zavian held himself. Something had rocked him to the core. Roshan took a swig of the coffee an attractive maid had given him upon arrival and slipped into his seat. He smiled at them both, covering his unease with his usual smoothness. "Apologies," he said. "I was delayed."

Zavian rolled his eyes. "Who was she?"

Roshan grinned. "I couldn't possibly divulge the name of the lady in question. I have her reputation to consider."

"I think her reputation must be the last thing on her mind if she decided to get together with you!"

Amir and Roshan laughed, but Zavian didn't. Roshan looked at Zavian and wondered what was going on. Amir looked suddenly thoughtful.

"You called the meeting, Zavian. What is so important

that you want us to get together, not two weeks since we last met?"

Roshan had never seen Zavian look so confused. Zavian opened his mouth to speak but closed it again as if he couldn't decide on the right words. Roshan suddenly felt a plunging in his stomach. He grimaced. It was worse than he'd first thought.

"Oh dear," he said, trying to keep his voice to its normal light tone. "This sounds serious."

Roshan glanced at Amir, but Amir's gaze was fixed on Zavian.

"It is serious," said Zavian. "I can no longer pursue marriage to Sheikha Elaheh of Tawazun."

Roshan slid down in the chair, letting his head fall against its back, and groaned. He opened his eyes slowly and stared at the dark ancient beams that intersected the whitewashed plaster ceiling. So it had come to this.

"Why?" asked Amir.

"Because my plans have changed."

Roshan couldn't stand it any longer. He jumped out of the seat and raked his fingers through his hair, twisting around to look at them both. He should have known the signs. "He's fallen in love."

Amir frowned and turned back to Zavian. "Zavian?" Amir asked, in a voice that doubted Roshan's assertion. "Is Roshan correct?"

Roshan had never seen Zavian look quite so afraid in all his life. But he guessed that love could do this to a man. Not that he had ever experienced it, nor did he ever intend to.

"Roshan is interpreting facts as they would pertain to him," said Zavian.

Roshan shook his head in mock despair and sat at the other end of the table. "I'm stating facts, Zavian, just as we've all ways agreed to."

"I've not fallen in love. I'm not in love." He flicked his hand in dismissal at the foolish notions. "These are romantic figments of your imagination, Roshan."

Roshan grunted. "Mine and the rest of the world. Except you, apparently."

"I repeat," Zavian said. "Love does not come into this. Is that statement enough for you?"

Roshan shrugged but wasn't convinced.

Amir held out a hand to stop the argument. "Whether you are, or are not, is of no importance here. What is of importance is that your plans have changed, and how that will impact us."

Zavian nodded and eyed each man in turn. "The marriage cannot proceed. I wish to marry another."

"I knew it!" Roshan exploded.

Watching Zavian try to find words to describe his feelings was painful. He stumbled on the word "need" and repeated it with emphasis. It seemed he'd found the right word. It was enough for Roshan.

"'You need her,'" repeated Roshan. "Whatever you call it, you're off the market, and so it falls to me." He swore under his breath.

"I can hardly be critical when I have done the same thing," said Amir. "Roshan? What do you think?"

"What do I think?" he asked with bitter emphasis. He shook his head and sighed. "I think that you have both lost your minds. That you have both put your personal happiness ahead of our three countries which comprise this land of ours." He rose and gripped the table, his tall frame casting a shadow over them both. "I think that it is as well that I, with all my reputation as a womanizer, set the least store by love. Because, Zavian, whatever you wish to call your requirement to wed this, whoever she is, don't fool yourself it isn't love." He sucked on a deep breath and pushed himself off the table. "Luckily for us all, I'm immune to such feelings. I adore women—plural— but fortunately, I don't love any particular one of them. Sheikha Elaheh of Tawazun will be as good as any to be my wife."

Zavian's face relaxed instantly, and he sat back in his chair with a relieved sigh. "Thank you, Roshan. And I'm sorry it has come to this, but there is nothing I can do about it."

Roshan looked from Amir to Zavian and shook his head in mock despair. "For all your alpha male machismo, you two are like putty in women's hands." Roshan ignored their insulted looks and continued. "While I might look like pretty putty on the outside, my strength is a steel heart. I know how to have fun, and I know how to keep myself safe." He looked from one to the other. "Leave it to me."

Amir and Zavian rose, and they all shook hands, but it was Roshan who left first. He walked briskly across the parched courtyard to the waiting helicopter. He didn't look back as the helicopter rose into the bright blue sky and turned east to his homeland.

He was the last choice to wed the sheikha for a reason. Marriage to the Sheikha of Tawazun was necessary to unite against their common enemy—the island nation of Jazira. And, out of the three of them, he hated Jazira the most. His parents had been killed by Jaziran mercenaries and he was therefore considered the weakest link in their joint armor against the enemy. But it seemed the strongest links had both been broken by love. Which left him. And he'd make damn sure the same thing wouldn't happen to him.

CHAPTER 1

The stretch limo swept around the circular drive in front of the palace. The impressive white building was lit from below with hundreds of footlights, giving the impression the palace was floating above the city. Exotically dressed people wearing masks—some beautiful, others grotesque—streamed up the steps leading to the magnificent white marble entrance, guarded by tall columns.

Shakira's excitement stepped up another notch as she scanned the scene from the limo. For the first time in forever, she was doing something just for herself, without interference from her family. It felt dangerous, it felt thrilling, it felt totally liberating.

She blushed as she looked down at what she was wearing. The skintight lacy black dress hadn't been her first choice, but her decision to attend the masquerade ball had been a late one, and there were few options at the hire store. It was far more revealing than she was comfortable with. Still, no one would ever know her identity, she reassured herself, looking out at the other masked party-goers.

Her brother thought she was here to do a job for him, but she wasn't. Sure, she'd go through the motions of following his command, but she'd already decided to follow her own agenda. Fun. That one word summed up the only thing she intended to get from this night. She had two days before she returned to the straitjacket confines of her country. Two days, she thought, with a sigh. It wasn't much time to pack in a lifetime's experiences before returning to the country she loved and an arranged marriage she didn't. But she refused to think of such things tonight.

She wound down the window as she waited in the queue of cars which lined the driveway, waiting to discharge their passengers. Music drifted out from the palace. She drank in the exotic glamor of the people in fancy dress, their identities disguised by elaborate masks. A flutter of nerves and excitement played in her stomach, and she checked her dark red lipstick in the mirror—the only part of her face revealed by the mask. Apart from her lips, the enigmatic gold mask remained fixed and inscrutable—the perfect disguise. Not that she needed one. She was raised in seclusion, far from the spotlight which lit the rest of her family.

When the limo finally rolled up to the steps, and it was her turn, she stepped carefully out of the car, ducking her head to prevent the feathers' tips that adorned her extravagant headgear from coming into contact with the limo's roof. She stood for a moment, checked her hair was still secured into a French twist, and drew in a deep breath, daunted by the prospect of walking up the steps in the high heels she rarely wore.

She focused so intently on managing the steps without stumbling that it wasn't until she walked through the entrance that she was suddenly aware that people were looking at her. Despite the extravagance of everyone else's clothes, people stopped talking and turned her way as she walked by. She felt their appreciation in every cell of her body, charging her with a thrilling sense of possibility.

Instinctively, her gait changed slightly, becoming more sensual in response to their interest in her figure-hugging dress, which left little to the imagination. While it was a far cry from her usual way of dressing, there was a part of her which she'd been suppressing for years that enjoyed being looked at.

She had grown up beside the beach, with the sun, sea, and sand next to her body, and was comfortable in her own skin. And it seemed that everyone else was comfortable looking at her barely concealed skin, too. Which was good because it would make her goal of enjoying a little innocent flirtation easier to achieve. Or not so innocent… if she was lucky.

She just had one little hurdle to cross first. She approached the palace official, and plucking the counterfeit invitation from her bag, handed it over to him. He barely glanced at it before smiling at her and placing the card in a basket with the others.

"*As-salam' alaykum.*" He gave the formal greeting with an informal twinkle in his eye.

"*Wa-alaykum as-salam,*" she replied.

"I hope you enjoy the ball, madam."

"I'm sure I will, thank you." She stepped away and thought she'd never spoken a truer word.

She accepted a flute of champagne from a passing waiter, who gave her a warm smile which she returned in full. Um, nice, she thought, appreciating the width of his shoulders and tight behind.

The thrill of danger tracked down her spine as she looked around for the man her brother had instructed her to target. She couldn't see him. When the decision had been made for her to attend the event, no one had known it would be a masquerade ball. But from what she knew of her target, he'd be easy to spot—tall, handsome, and incredibly arrogant. Maybe the gossip was correct, and he'd decided not to attend his own party. She hoped so. The only reason she wanted to identify the target was the opposite of her brother's—she wanted to avoid him.

She caught the waiter's eye again and smiled at his wink. Nothing wrong with a little flirtation to remind herself she was a woman. That was all it would be. Just a reminder of what her life had been like in England, where she'd been able—albeit temporarily—to be herself, an individual, not simply the only remaining daughter in a dysfunctional family. A little, sweet reminder before she returned to her family, her country, and her husband-to-be, who she hadn't even met. It wasn't much to ask, was it?

She took a sip of champagne, enjoying the effervescence of the liquid as it tickled her throat. Her senses seemed to be on high alert tonight, she thought, as she looked around. Despite that, she couldn't see her target. Looked like a no-show. She grunted. That would be like the man she'd heard so much about—a dilettante, an arrogant playboy, who was easily diverted by the next amusement, even before the first one had ended. A man not to be trusted.

She took a second, then a third sip, determined to shake off the remnants of inhibition, which made her self-conscious. Before she knew it, her glass was empty.

So, if he wasn't going to turn up, maybe it was time to enjoy herself. Now, where was that waiter? But she didn't have to look for the waiter after all as a couple of men came over and started talking to her. Business could wait. This girl was about to have a little fun.

"A SECURITY BREACH?" Roshan's brother, Xander, asked, his handsome face creasing slightly. According to one of Roshan's ex-girlfriends, women found Xander's saturnine good looks and narrow dark eyes incredibly sexy. Roshan couldn't see it. All he saw was a younger brother who preferred the world of finance to a world of politics and preferred to be anywhere else than Havilah. Preferably New York.

Roshan shrugged and turned his gaze back to the woman who he'd noticed as soon as she'd entered the room—he, along with all the other men. It would have been hard not to, given the transparency of the black dress, which barely covered her generous breasts and through which a G string was visible. The briefness of her dress contrasted with the impassive gold mask and the elaborate headdress. It spoke of sexiness and danger, not to mention a gorgeous body.

"It's probably nothing. A drone was seen flying over

the top of the palace. It disappeared before we could take it down."

Xander frowned. "What would our enemies want with photos of the palace's inner compound?"

Roshan shrugged again. "All knowledge is useful. Even if it's simply designed to undermine our feeling of security. Anyway, my team is looking into it and will report back by the end of the week."

"No sooner?"

"Apparently not. I've been assured it's nothing to be concerned about."

Xander grimaced slightly. "You need to beef up your security. I have a contact in the US who could help. He works at the cutting edge of security systems. Do you want me to run it by him?"

"We're not talking cutting edge here," said Roshan, with a shake of his head.

"I don't doubt it."

Roshan decided to ignore his brother's dismissal of the expertise in his country. Xander's belief that Havilah was a backwater compared to the rest of the world had always irked him. Still, he didn't want to waste time arguing with him, not when there were sexy women to flirt with. He watched two men join the gorgeous woman and begin chatting to her, as she finished her second glass of champagne. There was no time to waste. "I'm not rising to the bait tonight. There are more important things to focus on."

Xander followed his brother's gaze and grinned. "Perhaps I was a bit hasty in booking a flight back to the US tonight. Things are beginning to look interesting here."

Roshan practically growled at his brother. He was one

of the few who wasn't wearing a mask, as he'd only dropped in briefly to the party to say goodbye. And every woman's gaze lingered just a little longer on his darkly handsome face.

Xander held up his hand in surrender and laughing, replaced his half-drunk glass on the table. "Okay, she's all yours. I'm off before she sees me because you know, brother, that you wouldn't stand a chance next to me."

"Sure. It would be your humility which she'd find so attractive. Go away, Xander."

Xander laughed. "I will. I'll see you when I'm next needed here. Don't make it soon."

Roshan watched his enigmatic brother disappear, oblivious to the curious stares. Roshan adjusted his mask as he turned to look at the woman, whose full gold face mask gleamed in the dim lights. He was glad he'd insisted on wearing a different mask to the one everyone thought he was going to wear. He'd put out the word that he couldn't attend. He wanted to be incognito. He wanted a little fun tonight. Of course he had to marry, but both he and Sheikha Elaheh of Tawazun knew that their marriage had nothing to do with pleasure, but was all about business. And business could wait for another day.

Roshan began to weave his way around the party goers, stopping to test his disguise with a few people he knew by sight. There hadn't been any flicker of recognition. He looked at the sexy woman. He liked the idea that she wouldn't know his identity. It would be a good test to see if she liked him for who he was rather than what he was. He continued on to the beautiful woman who was drawing more men to her like bees to a honeypot.

He paused for a moment behind her, taking in the

honey brown of her skin and the slope of the neck, above which thick blonde hair was twisted up and under her headdress. He could tell she had fine bone structure by the clear line of her jaw and the delicacy of her collarbone. But she definitely wasn't skinny. Her shoulders appeared strong and athletic, and her waist narrow. Her bottom flared with a shapeliness which, as he moved around her, was reflected in the fullness of her breasts. She had an amazing figure.

He raised his eyes to her face as she slowly turned to face him. First to appear was the uplifted chin, the slice of jawline tempting him to run his finger around the rim of the mask; then the full impact of the gold mask—inscrutable and alluring—was revealed as she turned to face him; lastly his eyes rested on her lips. They were full, partly open, and painted in a deep, glossy red which sent suggestive ideas into his brain and other parts of his body which he tried hard to ignore. But then she smiled, and all bets were off. The smile was reflected in the warm flare of her eyes, which were of a dark, inviting, melting brown. He responded to their invitation with an answering smile.

He was gratified to see a flicker of response as her shoulders shivered as if something had tracked down her spine, and her breasts rose as she drew in a deep breath. It was all the more gratifying, knowing that there was no way she could recognize him. Her response was a purely animal one, and he was in the mood for animal.

"Good evening," he said.

She turned fully to him, signaling her interest. The other two men hung on, still hoping.

"Good evening to you," she said. Her voice was deep and husky. It spoke of cigarettes and drink and late nights.

His mind lingered on the late nights, going in a direction it really shouldn't be going in—not yet anyway. "Don't tell me," she said, leaning toward him. He was rewarded with an eyeful of cleavage. "You are the Joker."

"That's me," he said, instinctively echoing her stance. By moving in so close he could feel her warm breath against his neck. "But don't let it mislead you," he said. "I'm only a joker on the outside."

"Let me guess," she said, pressing her finger to his lips. He licked it lightly. It tasted of the champagne which had spilled from her glass. "And you're the devil, inside."

He couldn't help but smile. She'd hit the nail on the head. "Indeed. But I find it best to hide the real me. It frightens most people away."

"I'm not most people," she said.

"I sensed that," he said, his gaze unable to move from hers, despite her other obvious attractions. There was something intense and intriguing about their velvety depths. There was a lot more to this woman than a killer body. "But it's surely wise to fear the unknown."

"Hm," she grunted, a semi-orgasmic grunt which made his groin tighten with desire. "I'm curious about the unknown, I'm respectful of the unknown, but I'm not fearful of it. I don't frighten easily," she said, her long lustrous eyelashes suddenly visible as they dipped behind the gold mask.

Desire gripped him, as he wondered what expression lay behind that impassive beautiful gold mask. "Then your mask and headdress suit you," he said, glancing up at the elaborate feathered headdress. "Mata Hari," he murmured. "Interesting. She was an exotic dancer, a courtesan, and a spy." He paused, focusing on her eyes as he said each word, to see which one resonated. But there was no difference. Either none resonated, or they all did. "I wonder," he said, "what you are like on the inside, beneath that mask." He reached out and tugged the mask down slightly.

For a brief moment, he saw a flash of anger in her eyes as her hand clamped onto his and tossed it to one side. She nudged the mask back into place. Her eyes never left his. "A lady has her secrets," she said, her composure restored once more. "And they are to be revealed by invitation only."

He smiled and nodded. He'd received the message, loud and clear. He'd crossed a line. "I apologize. Curiosity got the better of me. But you must know that I always await an invitation. I am, after all, a cross between a joker and the devil. Neither, I believe, is insecure in themselves. And it is only someone insecure who takes what does not belong to them. I never do that."

Her dark eyes searched his, and then she nodded as if accepting his argument. "Good."

There was a sudden commotion at the door as a couple entered. She looked at them, and he followed her gaze and, for the first time, noticed that they were alone. His rival suitors had evidently picked up on the signals which were passing between the two of them, thickening the air with sensual innuendo.

"Who's that?" the beautiful woman asked, as the man who'd made the commotion at the entrance surveyed the party.

He gave the name of his friend, who always managed to act more preciously royal than he did.

"Oh," she said, sounding disappointed.

"Are you expecting someone?"

"No. I just thought it might be the king."

"You're interested in the king?"

Did he imagine it, or did that flick of the tongue between those beautiful red lips betray uncertainty? She quickly smiled, and he forgot his suspicions. "Just curious."

"Have you met him?"

"No. But I've heard a lot about him."

"Anything good?"

Those slender but strong shoulders shrugged. "Good, bad, and everything in between."

Roshan shifted uncomfortably, knowing he should change the subject but curious to discover precisely how strangers—particularly beautiful strangers—perceived him. "Bad? Surely not?"

Those beautiful lips clamped tight for a moment as if she'd swallowed something distasteful. "Some of the ways the king and his countrymen treat their neighboring countries is quite brutal, I hear."

He was glad he could hide his surprised response behind the mask. He took a sip of champagne to give himself time to recover. "Really? In what way?"

She shook her head and smiled. "Just hearsay."

He recovered slightly. "I'm sure he's not as bad as the hearsay makes out."

"Are you?"

How had he got himself into a situation where he was defending himself to a stranger while pretending to be someone else?

"Yes," he said, beckoning over a waiter. He needed another drink. "Because it's his party and he's very free with the champagne. And that is a sign that he is a very good man." He gave her what he hoped was both a winning smile and one which would put an end to that particular subject. "Would you care for another drink?"

Her lush deep red lips worked at the corners, and while he would not take such liberties as to kiss them, his imagination knew no similar bounds.

"No, thank you," she replied. "Two drinks are all I ever allow myself. I like to keep a clear head at all times."

He frowned slightly. "You're not a doctor, someone on duty?"

The quirked lips fell back into place again. His frown deepened.

"No, I'm not a doctor," she said with that superbly husky voice. "I'm simply a woman who likes to be aware of everything that goes on. Everything around me and everything to do with me. Why would I want to dull my sensations?"

It was his turn to smile. "I agree. The dulling of sensations should be the province of the dull. And I do believe you're not that."

She smiled in response, revealing even white teeth and the tip of a pink tongue. Again, a shiver of desire ran through his body. And again, he had to repress it. He knew from their short acquaintance that this woman, Mata Hari, or whoever she was, would make the running, and he would follow.

"I've been accused of many things, but never of being dull." She tapped his chest with her forefinger. It did nothing to control the desire. It turned the shiver into a full-on solid thing that refused to be ignored. He just hoped it could be controlled. "If you're wondering what I was looking for as I was looking around, it was for some fresh air."

She hadn't been in the room long enough to get hot, he thought. Nor was she wearing enough to feel the heat. But he wasn't about to argue with her. The masquerade ball was an annual event for charity, not something he would miss.

"You know, I was thinking the same thing." He wasn't, but he certainly was now. "And I think I know of a place we can go."

She looked him up and down, and he felt his body react as if her eyes were lasers heating his eyes, his chin, his chest, and lower and then back again. He could have sworn he held his breath as he waited for her response. When it came, it was a simple nod. She had agreed, but to what, he had yet to find out.

CHAPTER 2

She certainly needed fresh air—preferably icy cold air that would sweep away the dense cloud of sexuality, which enveloped them both. She'd come here wanting fun, and it looked like she'd found someone who was more than willing to join her in that fun. But she couldn't help wondering if she'd bitten off more than she could chew. This man oozed sensuality, flirtation, and a macho sense of knowing exactly what he wanted to do to her. This man was made for pleasure.

Heavens, she thought as she felt the heat of his hand against the small of her back, barely covered by the black lace, as he guided her to a set of French doors which opened out onto the rear palace gardens. She'd wanted a dalliance, and she'd certainly got one. And what a one!

Every gesture, every movement of his broad shoulders and tall, lean figure, had her body responding. It was purely instinctive. And, after two years of study cut short by her brother's demands, she welcomed instinct over intellect. She'd had enough of over-thinking everything, and she'd certainly had enough of doing what her family told her to do. Every part of her wanted to rebel against her brother's requirement for duty, against her need to be careful, always to place her desires second, or third to others.

One glance at the stranger by her side made her realize that, for once, her needs coincided with those of her companion.

Just one night, she promised herself. That would be all. A night of sensation to remember in the coming days and weeks when she'd have to once more suppress herself for the sake of her family and the country she loved more than anything. No one would know. Just this man—this stranger, this joker—who would know no more about her than she knew about him.

He guided her past the terrace where people had spilled out from the party to listen to traditional music, its haunting sound a contrast to the modern western music playing inside the palace.

She stopped and turned to the musicians, entranced by the music she hadn't heard since she'd left her homeland. It took her back to when she was a child—not too far from here—when she'd snuck into late-night parties and listened to the music her grandparents had enjoyed.

She gave a light gasp at the sudden, unexpected memory which tore at her, viscerally, and blinked back the tears. None of that past remained—it had all gone.

"Are you okay?" asked her companion, whose name she still didn't know, and whose name she fully intended never to know.

"Sure."

"Did you want to stay and listen to the music?"

She smiled at the polite question. Whoever this devil was, he was considerate, not demanding that they act on their undeniable urges. He was letting her take the lead, just as he'd implied earlier.

She gave one last glance at the musicians and stepped away. That was the past, and one she could never recover. All she wanted at this moment was the present, and new memories to store up for the future.

She shook her head and turned to drink in his sensual lips and the promise he held in his body. "No, I'd prefer to go somewhere more private."

His smile shone white in the dim light, and he took her hand in his. "I think I know just the place."

They walked alongside the rectangle of dark green water upon which the solar lamps which edged the pathway were reflected. The path took them across the courtyard, and she soon found herself at the opposite end of the garden to the party.

Here, sounds were muted by the graceful leafy boughs of the overhanging trees and luxuriant growth of fragrant flowers and climbers which clung to the colonnaded walkway. Only the ancient sounds of the Bedouin instruments reached them, like fingers from the past, poking at her memories.

She looked around, wanting to escape further. She wanted no reminders of who she was. A few people lingered amongst the foliage, engaged in private—and in some cases, very private—conversation. Her devil paused at a wooden gate and put his hand on the latch as if to open it. She looked around, wondering if they'd be stopped by one of the security guards she'd spotted along the way.

"Are you allowed in there?"

He squeezed her hand and brought it to her lips and kissed it. A shiver of desire coursed down her back and settled deep inside of her. She swallowed.

"What can they do if they catch us?" His voice was deep, its timbre stimulating her ears and skin as if it were a tangible thing. She sucked in a deep breath. He glanced at her rising breasts. The flimsy stuff of her bra couldn't disguise her peaked nipples, which betrayed her desire. "Would they dare to throw out the Joker and Mata Hari?" he added. "We make a daunting couple, I think."

And for one long moment, she imagined what her life could have been like if she'd been born in a different country, to a different family. She could have been one half of a "daunting" couple; she could have been carefree and simply alive, like she felt now; she could have been truly herself. But she had now. May be it was all that she had.

"Good point," she said. "Lead the way." She took another deep breath and knew that what she was about to do was so unlike anything else she'd ever done before, that it would create a memory like no other. It was dangerous, it was foolhardy, and she couldn't wait. She was ready for whatever was about to happen.

ROSHAN PUT his hand on the wooden bar to open the door and hesitated, glancing up at the security cameras he knew were hidden amongst the trees. He gave a slight nod and felt the response under his hand as the latch released its hidden mechanism, and he was allowed entry. He might like to fool with the rest of the palace and guests, but he always made sure his security team knew his identity. As he'd implied to the beauty by his side, he was only a joker on the surface.

His Mata Hari appeared reassured by the ease of entrance to the inner gardens. She stepped ahead of him and looked around. He followed her gaze to the intimate garden, which was for his private use. Three sides of the courtyard gave entrance to his suite of rooms—not that his guest would realize that—and the fourth was a high wall, topped with tumbling vines and leaves, which divided it from the formal outer courtyard.

It was darker in this inner garden, and the music and laughter and hum of conversation was barely heard now. The only lights came from the stars above, which shone brightly on this moonless night. All he had to do was take her across the gardens, and he would be in his bedroom. But he didn't always do what he wanted, not straight away. Where would be the fun in that?

Instead, he stopped at a daybed, nestled under a pergola overhanging with fragrant plants. It was deep and cushioned—perfect for outside adventures, as well as for times when he wished to be alone and to think. But thinking wasn't on his mind right at that moment.

His Mata Hari took a few paces forward and then turned to look at him when he didn't walk beyond the daybed. Her gold mask and luscious red lips caught the starlight, and he sucked in a breath. He hoped she didn't wish to walk any further because he was hard and ready for her, just holding her hand. He wanted her here and now.

She tilted her head to one side as if in query, her feathered headdress brushing his face. "We are the only ones here," she said. "Why is that?"

"Perhaps because the others are performing courtship rituals which we have circumnavigated." He paused. For a moment, he wondered if he'd misread the signals. Then she smiled, walked over to him, ran her finger along his jawline, and flicked his chin.

"I think the devil inside," she said provocatively, "has just made an appearance."

He slipped his hands around her waist and drew her closer to him. "I think you're right."

She lifted her face to his, the gold of her mask, all he could see, outshining the dark luster of her eyes. "The thing about me you don't know," she said, her breath hot against his mouth, "is that I'm always right." With that, she rose slightly on balls of her feet and pressed her lips to his.

He readied himself to hold himself back, to accept what he anticipated to be a teasing glancing kiss. But he'd forgotten that it was Mata Hari he was dealing with. This was no brush of the lips, but a full-on assault.

She kissed him hungrily as if she'd been craving the lips and touch of a man her whole life. He responded with equal fervor. He hadn't been waiting his whole life to kiss a woman. In fact, he'd just spent a very agreeable two weeks with one in Paris, but this woman was a force of nature he had no intention of trying to withstand.

As her tongue plunged into his mouth and met his in a swirling, sweeping caress, he felt her groan emerge from her mouth and move into his. At the same time, her soft, lush curves rested against his, ready for him.

He knew the moment she'd registered his erection because she pressed her hips harder against him. He kept her there, his hands caressing the scanty lace which covered her bottom as she rubbed up against him. It was as if she was desperate for him, and that desperation was completely reciprocated. He could think of nothing else now.

When they finally drew apart, they were breathless with lust. She pressed her cheek against his chest, and he held her close as she trembled in his arms. Then she carefully adjusted her mask, which had shifted out of place. It seemed she wanted to continue to be incognito. That, too, was fine by him.

She smiled, her lipstick smudged over her swollen lips, and placed both palms against his bare chest—his shirt somehow having become undone under her quick fingers. Then she pushed him, and he sat down on the day bed, more than happy for her to take the lead.

He leaned back on his hands and looked up at her. "You might want to remove your headdress. I fear the canopy will knock it off, otherwise."

She looked up, acknowledged the truth of his suggestion with a shrug, quickly unpinned the feathered confection, and placed it on a nearby bench. She shook out long, thick, blonde hair, and came over to him.

He held his breath as he wondered what she'd do next. Because one thing was for sure, if she wanted to take control, he wouldn't stop her. He didn't have to wait long to find out.

She raised one knee, the stretchy stuff of her dress

restricting her movements only a little, and placed it on the bed, and then raised the other and knelt above him. She placed one hand either side of his shoulders, and he was rewarded with the sight of the top of her impressive breasts. It was his turn to groan.

Her gold mask loomed over him. It was menacing and ridiculously erotic. While the impassive mask, dark eyes, and full red lips hovered over him, framed by her cloud of hair, he drew his hands up from her calves, caught her dress, and pulled it up her hips. He caressed her bare bottom and watched to see if she would remove her mask and reveal herself. But it seemed that still wasn't her intention.

Instead, she levered herself up and stood up above him, pulling down her G string as that mask, those eyes, continued to search his Joker-like face for similar clues, no doubt. But there were other parts of his body that quite clearly revealed his reaction, and it was a reaction which only strengthened beneath her lingering gaze.

She shuddered with desire and lifted first one knee, wriggled out of her G string, and then the other knee and flicked it to one side.

He pushed up her dress until it lay in a ruffle around her small waist. Her light chocolate skin gleamed in the starlight. He breathed in her fragrance, and his mouth watered as his hands swept up her thighs and came to rest on her hips. She had one knee either side of his hips, and then she sat back on her haunches and swept up her hands over his stomach and chest. He breathed in sharply and fell back on the cushions as he succumbed to the feel of her hands and breath against his skin. He reached out to touch her mask. He wanted it off now. He wanted to know her now. But she pulled away.

"Later," she said, her voice two shades huskier. "I want to give you pleasure first."

He swallowed, trying to focus on her words, while her hands stripped his brain of sense. "You don't want pleasure?" he asked, his voice, rough with lust.

"Oh," she said. "I fully intend to have pleasure. I gain pleasure by giving it, as well as receiving it."

"A courtesan, then," he said. "Your Mata Hari is a courtesan," he elaborated.

"You cannot reduce me to one thing," she said. "I am many. Some hidden, some not."

He didn't doubt it. Any further thoughts fled as he succumbed to her touch against his stomach, as she pulled aside his shirt and then swept her fingers inside the waistband of his trousers. His stomach jumped at the touch allowing her fingers to drive further and touch the top of his erection.

She jolted up with a start and, with renewed excitement, undid his button and fly and pushed away his clothes, taking hold of him with both hands. She explored his length before he lifted his hips and she pulled down his trousers to his knees. She swept them onto the ground, on top of her G string.

Then she brought those beautiful, smudged red lips down on him, and all thought fled as he closed his eyes and succumbed to the magic of her lips, her tongue, her mouth, enveloping and exploring him. She only briefly lifted herself from him before sensuously rolling on a condom she must have retrieved from her bag.

Suddenly she rose and, with her golden face mask still

in place, lowered herself onto him centimeter by tiny centimeter. He could see the fluttering tips of her eyelashes under her golden mask. Her rapidly rising and falling breasts and the pulse he could feel in her wrist as he held her hand, were all that betrayed her lust and reaction as she slid slowly onto him.

Once she was on him fully, she stilled and arched her back. She tilted her head up to the midnight sky, and the gold mask shone in the starlight, which found entry through the branches of the tree above them.

She wriggled on him and shivered, giving herself pleasure with each small movement. With both their masks intact, it felt as if there were no connection between them, as if she were using him. It was a strange feeling—to be separate and yet so connected.

He gripped her other hand, wanting her to come closer to him. She looked down then, and the gold darkened—dark eyes and the darkness of her open mouth. A thrill of the unknown lapped over him. And then she rose from him slowly. All thoughts of separateness left him as he closed his eyes and surrendered to the bliss of her body around his, caressing him, massaging him. If she wanted to take control, he knew it would also give him pleasure.

She continued to rise and fall on him, picking up the tempo, her breathing coming faster, until she suddenly cried out—the sound muffled as she fell against him, the gold mask cool against his chest. It was as if she had suddenly become vulnerable, and he put his arms around her and held her. It was a strange feeling—as if he'd known her for a long time and wanted to protect her.

The moment passed, and she rose and looked at him. She wriggled slightly, and that was the signal. With one swift movement, he'd flipped her onto her back with him above her. It was his turn now, and he was going to make sure he could do what he wanted. With a thumb under each corner of the face mask, he lifted it gently from her face and pulled it away over the top of her head. She didn't demur. He had been half-afraid of some deformity, but her face was as beautiful as her body. Large, wide brown eyes, high cheekbones, and her bruised, lush lips—all set in a perfect oval. She was stunning.

It was the last thought as his lips found hers in a kiss that was all the more passionate now there were no barriers between them. Their tongues tangled, and their breaths merged and panted, as he controlled her with his hips. With his arms tight around her, he thrust into her repeatedly, driving them both to the point of annihilation where bliss existed.

They rolled to their side and continued to kiss, still connected. It was as if they couldn't get enough of each other. As if the first orgasm was merely the entrée, a taste of what else was in store. He couldn't wait for the dessert.

From the previous sense of disconnection, he now felt quite the opposite, as if he were one with her. The sensation was novel. He couldn't recall ever having experienced a feeling of being something more than himself. He felt at the same time both lost and yet, paradoxically, found. How could that be?

But he had no time to ponder the strange feelings which had overtaken him, because she was rubbing against him, her legs around his hips, him still inside of her, urging him on. He needed no further urging, and their love-making continued, at a different level, less urgent and more exploratory. Now, after the first pressing demands of lust had been satisfied, they could take the time to explore each other's bodies—licking, nipping, fingertips upon fingertips, legs sliding upon legs— relishing in the sensations of each other's skin and curves.

When they came together this time, it was different yet again—less extreme and yet deeper somehow. The annihilation was complete, he thought to himself as they rolled on their backs, and their breathing slowly returned to normal.

It was far more than Shakira had imagined. The intensity of the pleasure lingered in every part of her body. Her brain and heart were stilled in the ensuing silence—satisfied, replete, at peace.

But suddenly, the silence was pierced by a ringtone coming from her bag. For a moment, they stared at each other—strangers engaged in the most intimate act—and the full implication of what she'd just done, just how far she'd got carried away, hit her like the sudden deluge of a monsoon on a broiling day.

The ringtone pierced the silence once more, and she moved away from him, sitting up and pushing her fingers through her hair. She scrambled off the bed and plucked the phone from her bag, tugging at her dress as she fumbled with the phone, nearly dropping it, she was shaking so much. The brightness of the screen pierced the shadows and brought her back to her senses. What had she done?

She quickly read the message. Her brother wanted an

update, and she had none to give—not what he was wanting and expecting, anyway.

She picked up her headdress and mask, knowing that it was time to leave. The spell had been broken. But a part of her didn't want to leave behind this moment, not without a memento anyway. With her phone in her hand, she turned to the empty bed upon which they'd just made love and took a photo, turned, and took another one. She wanted to be able to revisit this moment at any time in the future when her future looked dim.

"What are you doing?" He stood partially clothed beside the bed, his face still in the shadows.

She turned to him and pocketed her phone. "Just something to remember our evening by."

"Has our evening finished already?"

She nodded regretfully. "Yes, I must go."

He got out his own phone and took a photo of her. "Then I will also have something to remember our evening by."

"I must go," she repeated. "My… taxi will be waiting for me."

He took hold of her shoulders and squeezed her gently and sensuously, and for an instant, she was back with him, attuned to his body, her body, his to command.

"Stay," he said. Oh, but she wanted to. His hands slid lower down her arms before coming to rest on her hands, which he brought to his lips and kissed. "Why don't you stay the night with me," he asked, as if realizing his first word sounded like an order. "We can do whatever you like—make love, talk, eat, sleep. Just stay and do all of those things with me."

She hesitated and licked her lips, as if the thought of what he offered had made her hungry. And she was. He'd given her pleasure like she'd never had before, and she knew, without a doubt, that he would give her more. If she were an ordinary person, she'd jump at the chance. But she wasn't, was she?

She shook her head. "I can't," she said, trying hard to summon a smile, but it refused to remain on her face. "Besides, we can hardly stay here. I think the palace guards might have something to say about that! I doubt we should even be here."

"Don't worry about the guards." He pushed back her hair from her face and moved until the starlight lit his features, and she saw the whole of him without the mask for the first time. He'd only taken off his mask immediately before they made love. And then she'd seen his lips and eyes, as she'd gone to kiss them, but not the whole face.

And she knew that face.

She cleared her throat as she tried to suppress the knowledge which she dared not consider. "And why shouldn't the guards worry?"

She stepped further into the pale starlight, wanting him to do the same. He followed, drawn by their joined hands.

He sighed. "Take my word for it, they won't."

She turned away and looked around her. "And where do you propose we should stay the night?" Slowly she turned and faced him. "Here, in the palace?"

He smiled as if pleased she'd only just realized who he was. Of course, it was some kind of game to him. He was no doubt tired of people wanting to sleep with him because he was king—the Playboy King—that was what people called him.

She would never have had sex with him if she'd known who he was. She'd wanted something to remember when she was trapped in the confines of her country, married to someone she could never love for the sake of a country she loved too much.

He pulled on his trousers and smiled at her. He drew his thumb down her cheek, lifting her chin, so she was forced to look at him. "Yes, here." He gestured to the rooms. "My rooms."

She swept her arm, indicating the palace rooftops. "Your palace," she said slowly. He frowned. She twisted away from him, grabbed her bag, and stepped away. She let her hair tumble around her face and shoulders, in the vain hope that it would conceal her face. Not that he'd know her identity. Her ultra-conservative father had always kept her well away from the public eye. She gripped the bag and held it between them as if for defense. "I have to go."

She couldn't risk talking to him anymore. She didn't trust herself and, before he could say anything further, she began to walk away. The walk turned into a swift run, and she quickly found herself at the wooden door, which now miraculously sprang open. She glanced up and saw what she hadn't seen earlier—cameras. Not, she realized with relief, trained on the bed where they'd made love, but on whoever entered and exited. What she'd thought was an easily opened door had been opened remotely for him.

She ran across the gardens and slipped out to the front steps and found her taxi waiting for her. She jumped inside, and the taxi drove off quickly. As it drove by the entrance, she caught sight of the man she'd just left—the playboy king, the devil—both were apt names. He stood on the steps, hands on hips, his shirt partially untucked, looking down at her as the taxi swept by. Their eyes met briefly—his confusion framed by a frown—before she was gone, driving back down the hill into the city where she could become anonymous once more.

As he watched his Mata Hari drive by, her hair still in disarray, her full lips impossibly sexy with the smeared remnants of the lipstick, he wondered what the hell had happened. He'd had the most incredible love-making he'd ever experienced with someone who didn't even know his identity. And yet, when she knew who he was, she couldn't get away fast enough.

He stood for a few moments, watching the tail lights of her taxi disappearing into the city below them. He'd wanted to know what it was like to be with a woman who didn't know his identity. It seemed his status as king wasn't such a drawcard as he'd always imagined. The notion should have pleased him. But here, now, with her gone, it had the opposite effect.

Instead, he felt a sense of panic. He was accustomed to being in control of his world, but the one person he wanted to spend time with had just disappeared, and he had no idea who she was or where she was going. He turned to one of the guards. "The taxi which just left, gets its registration from the security cameras. I want to know its destination."

He returned inside, feeling bereft after the intimacy which had been more than physical, which had been unique. There was nothing more he could do that night. But in the morning he knew he would have the destination of the taxi and the identity of the woman who had just pivoted his world onto a different axis.

A woman he could only think of as Mata Hari, as he had no clue as to her real identity—not her name or anything else about her. But despite her anonymity, he knew that he would not be able to put her out of his mind for the rest of the night. And beyond.

CHAPTER 3

Shakira moved the phone from one ear to the other and looked out over the city's rooftops. She continued to listen to her brother's tirade, her dark eyes becoming opaque and steely with each passing insult.

"What do I mean? I mean, Nabeel, exactly what I say. I didn't succeed."

She paced the floor, one arm across her waist, and the other holding the phone to her ear, counting each tile. When had Nabeel begun to rant rather than talk normally? She couldn't remember when the change had occurred. It must have been a gradual one, just as his slip into drugs and alcoholism had been.

Nabeel had always been fearless, just as she was, but his fearlessness was no longer moderated by judgment— that had been impaired by the megalomania brought on by his addictions. There was no longer any doubt about it: her brother had become a liability, both as a brother and king.

She suddenly realized she didn't need to continue

listening to Nabeel, and, with a brief touch of the screen, the ranting stopped. She tossed the phone on the bed but continued to pace across the cool, tiled floor from one side of the large room to the other. The sounds and smells of the city street below her drifted up into her room. The windows were wide open, and she'd turned the air conditioning off. She liked to connect with her world, not be sealed away from it, like Nabeel.

Nabeel. She should never have agreed to his command. She should never have come on this fool's errand. She paused in front of the window and looked across the city to the palace. Even while she wished she'd disobeyed her brother, she knew, deep down, that she could never regret how her evening had ended.

What had begun as a rebellion against Nabeel and what he was forcing her to do, had turned into an experience she was never going to forget. Her connection to the king had been instant and genuine, and their lovemaking had been exquisite. Just the thought of what he'd done to her and how he'd made her feel sent a shiver of desire through her body. She couldn't hate this man she was born to hate. She simply couldn't summon it up. He was sexy, sweet, smart, and funny. He was not a killer of her people—of that she was sure. Maybe his father had been, but not this man.

Her brother's requirements of her, and her own needs, had collided, coming together in that one person—Sheikh Roshan al-Haidar, King of Sharq Havilah. She may have been sent on a fool's errand and been determined not to be that fool. But she ended up being one anyway.

Suddenly a knock at the door ended her ruminations. She looked through the peephole, and her heart nearly stopped. It was him. Roshan. Should she open the door? She probably shouldn't, but the thought was swiftly forgotten as she found herself opening the door to him.

He stood with one arm casually propped against the doorjamb, the other holding a picnic basket.

"Care for a picnic?" he asked.

All the things which were piling into her mind to say to him evaporated. If he had said anything else, she thought she would have exploded, angry that he had tracked her down and had found her. As she contemplated her response, laughter exploded on her lips.

"I wasn't sure what you liked," he continued.

"There's a reason for that," she said, crossing her arms. "And that's because we don't know each other."

He raised a sexy eyebrow. "We know some parts of each other extremely well," he said. Behind him, the elevator pinged and the door slid open, and a couple walked out. "I seem to remember when you –"

She didn't wait for him to elaborate but grabbed his arm, as the couple walked by with their faces turned inquisitively toward them, and pulled him into her room.

Roshan dropped the basket to the floor and walked across the room. He stood by the window looking out at the city, which she knew now to be his. He turned at the sound of her closing the door behind her.

"I wondered how I could get into your room." He smiled. "I didn't imagine embarrassment would have done it. Not after last night. I didn't think you are the kind to be easily embarrassed."

"Being embarrassed and being humiliated are two very different things."

His smile faded, and he sat on the corner of the couch. "It was not my intention to humiliate you."

"What do you wish to do then?"

"I wish to be in your company." He nodded at the wicker basket. "I know a perfect place for a picnic by the sea, and I thought you would be the perfect person to share it with me. And, at the same time, I might find out your name."

"You tracked me down to the hotel. I'm sure you know my name by now."

He rose from the chair and walked over to her. "I know the name you gave hotel reception, but that surely isn't your real name."

She tried to suppress a smile. "Mata Hari. True." Before she could move, he had dipped his head and pressed his lips to hers in a brief but telling kiss. She wanted more, and there was no way she wasn't going on this picnic. Before she could reach out to him, he had moved past her and picked up the basket once more. He opened the door and held it open for her. She plucked her bag off the bed and went through the door, and he followed her. In the elevator, he kissed her again, this time with more intensity. She had half a mind to return to her bedroom.

But she wanted to play his game, because she had a feeling that the waiting would be as enjoyable as the consummation.

He was nothing like she'd imagined him to be. She had two days more in his country, and there was no way she was going to spend that time being her brother's pawn. She would spend that time doing exactly as she pleased.

And it pleased her to be with Roshan. *He* pleased her very much.

As Roshan put the Ferrari into gear and stole a glance at the woman by his side—a woman whose name he still did not know—he thought it had been easier than he'd imagined. He knew very little about her. But he knew she was a woman who only did what she wanted. All he had to do was to make sure that what she wanted was what he wanted. And, luckily, it seemed he had done just that.

They wanted each other, but they wanted the fun of the chase as well. And he knew all about the chase. He'd spent his whole life studying it. If there is one thing he was an expert on, it was flirtation and lovemaking. But he'd never come across anyone quite like this woman.

He could have her here and now. He knew she wanted him as much as he wanted her. He could see it in her dark eyes, in the sensual twist of her mouth and in the way she sat, angled towards him. He forced his mind to switch to other things. He didn't want to get ahead of himself.

"Am I allowed to know your name?"

She didn't say anything for several moments as she watched the cityscape disappearing. Then she turned to him. "Shakira."

"Shakira," he said, tasting the sound of her name on his tongue. It tasted good. "That's a pretty name."

She grunted. "It's a common name. My parents wanted another boy. They were disappointed to have a girl. They didn't put much effort into the choosing of my name. My nanny chose it for me."

Roshan nodded as he took in her words, realizing it

was probably the most she'd spoken to him in the short time they'd known each other. It changed the frame of her —gave her a setting. He reframed his image of her and took a shot.

"You have brothers then?" he asked.

She looked back out through the window. "Only one now," she said softly. "And not the best of them."

Again, a reframing. Not merely an alluring woman, but a woman with a tragic past. He didn't want tragic; he wanted easy. She was determined to make it difficult for him—to stab at the hard, calcified thing other people called his heart.

"I'm sorry to hear that."

She shrugged, the movement reminiscent of the previous night. His body responded accordingly. He shifted his attention back again to the here and now.

"I, too, have a brother—younger, and also not the best of us." He grinned. "By contrast to him, I seem modest."

She turned to him with an answering smile, which revealed two dimples in her cheeks. "That I would like to see!"

He didn't like the thought of introducing this wonderful woman to his charming brother. "No way. I've never been good at sharing my toys."

She raised an eyebrow. "And is that how you see me? A toy?"

He swept his eyes over her, and a barely suppressed groan emerged from his lips. He licked his lips and focused straight ahead on the road. "Truthfully? Yes, at the moment, that's all I know about you. You're beautiful, sexy as hell, and"—he glanced her way briefly once more —"you're enigmatic. I know nothing more about you.

That's why I asked you to come with me this morning. I want to know more about you. I want you to become more than a toy to me."

Did he imagine the shadow which passed over her eyes as she turned a frowning face to look out at the passing scenery? He must have done because when she turned back to him, the frown had vanished. But her face remained serious. "Do I have any say in this?"

"You have all the say."

She nodded, and the sweet curve of her lips emerged once more. "Good. Because I quite like the idea of playing with you like a toy. I'm not sure I want to know you any better than that."

He shot her a surprised glance. "Your wish is my command."

She grunted and sat back in her seat. "Has anyone ever told you that you're incorrigible?" she asked.

"Indeed. And I'm sure you have had the same accusation leveled at you."

The dimpled smile turned into a laugh. "Life's too short to be corrigible."

He raised an eyebrow in query.

She shook her head. "Haven't a clue what 'corrigible' means either. I only know I have no wish to be it." She cast a restless glance around the opening countryside. "It sounds far too dull."

"Exactly my thoughts."

"And yet you're king," she said thoughtfully, turning to face him again. "Don't you have a duty to be dull?"

Her words struck him where it hurt. He'd been rebelling against the notion his whole life. He cleared his throat and overtook a car, pushing his foot flat to the floor, the car easing into the increased speed, finding the new speed more to its liking. He glanced into his rearview mirror. He could still see his security keeping a discreet distance behind the car he'd just overtaken. Only then, after his initial response had faded, did he answer.

"I have a duty to be king. And I am. But I am also a person with my own needs and desires, and to deny these would make me a worse king."

She grunted in agreement. "I guess so. But that must be quite the balancing act."

"I'd rather talk about you," he said, needing to change the subject. Again, she'd hit the nail on the head. Every minute of every day was like a balancing act to him—trying to keep focused on the business of running his country, while trying to satisfy his restless nature. "What brings you to my country?"

Did her shoulders stiffen slightly? Her profile was three-quarters, and her eyes hidden by her sunglasses. "Oh, I came to see someone, but it didn't work out."

"His, or her, loss, is my gain," he said, with a degree of satisfaction. "And I hope yours. Have you ever seen the Havilah Sha'ab reef at close quarters? The majority of it is in foreign waters, but at least we have the best of it."

"No, I've never swum on it, but I adore swimming, and I go every minute I can when I'm at home." It was like the last word was bitten off—as if it had escaped before she could stop it. She looked sharply away from him.

He knew she'd just revealed something important, but for the life of him, he couldn't imagine what. He signaled and made a left turn down a rutted track, a barrier rising as the sentry guards recognized him.

"And where is home?"

"I've just finished studying in London."

It wasn't an answer to his question, but it seemed it was all he was getting. He didn't press her. He'd find out sooner or later where her home was. From her accent and complexion, he knew it couldn't be far from his own country. Then why wasn't she telling him?

"Well, you're in luck with this beach. The water is clear and warm. Unfortunately, much of our reef is out of reach."

"*Our* reef?"

"My people regard it as theirs but it was won in battle, at great cost, by Jazira decades ago. We can only swim on a part of it. Still, it's a pristine part of the coast, and there's not a soul to share it with." He glanced in his rearview mirror. "Except a dozen or so security guards, but they'll come no closer. This entire stretch of beach is off-limits to the public. We're safe here to do whatever we please."

They exchanged looks, and he knew that, once more, they were of like mind. And that mind more than compensated for any reluctance to tell him about herself.

Once he'd parked the car, Shakira leaped out. He watched as she walked over to the shore, where small waves broke on the white sand. She glanced around at the sheltering cliffs, then stripped off her clothes, leaving only her bra and G string, ran out into the water and dived in. Roshan placed the picnic baskets on a table beneath the palm trees, pulled off his clothes, and followed her in.

Shakira swam briskly out towards the pontoon. She'd twisted her hair into a knot on top of her head and pounded through the choppy waves with ease. He swam swiftly and soon caught her up. He followed her up onto the pontoon which overlooked the reef, and looked around, trying not to be seduced by the vision of her lying flat on her back, her eyes closed. He couldn't help being reminded of a shark basking in the bright sunlight. She was as beautiful and as dangerous.

"Mmm," she groaned, pulling one knee up and placing her hands under her head, her eyes still firmly closed. "It's good to get back into the sea again. It feels ages since I've swum."

He turned to her, his interest piqued once more. "You haven't been home in a while, then?"

He could have kicked himself as she rolled onto her stomach and laid her cheek on her crossed arms. His gaze raked her body before pulling away. He sat down beside her, studiously trying to avoid looking at her barely covered bottom.

"I've been busy."

"You should never be too busy for pleasure," Roshan said. "And that's your ruler speaking."

She twisted her head onto her other cheek to face him. "You're not my ruler," she said quietly, her voice husky now.

"I am while you're in my country," he said, equally quietly.

She leaned on her elbow and supported her head on her hand.

"Is that so?" Her full lips quirked at the corners, revealing those adorable dimples. He closed his eyes and lifted his face to the sun.

"That's right. I am the king, and you have to do everything I say."

Her laughter filled the bay and wriggled deep inside of him. He didn't move.

"And I command you to stop laughing," he said mildly.

She rolled onto her back, still laughing. She jumped up as her laughter died and stood looking at him, her hands on her hips, her luscious body looming over him. He marveled at its sensual perfection. The marveling turned into something much more physical, which, as her eyes dropped to his hips, he realized she'd noticed.

She knelt beside him, and he held his breath as he felt her gaze rake his body. And when her eyes met his once more, he knew that she was similarly roused.

She placed her hands close to his body. Her mouth was close to his, so close that he could feel her warm breath against his cheek. Her breasts brushed against his chest. It was the perfect moment between desire and satiation when he felt hyper-aware of everything—the beating sun, the brisk breeze, and her presence: her perfume, her proximity, her hair grazing his shoulder. Perfect.

And then she came closer still and touched the side of his body, sending shivers of desire across his skin. She wriggled her fingers further around him and then, with one swift movement, rolled him off the pontoon and into the water.

The cold water slapped against his heated, roused body with the force of an insult. But he, too, had grown up in the water and immediately dived down and came around the other side, and when she extended a hand to pull him up, he pulled her in with a cry and a splash. She tried to swim away, but he grabbed her ankle and pulled her back to him. A mouthful of water subdued her cry, and she spluttered, laughing, as he pulled her towards him, her body bumping against his.

She put her hands on his shoulders as they both trod water.

"Are you trying to drown me?" she asked.

"No, I'm trying to punish you," he lied. Punishment was the furthest thing from his mind.

Her smile faded, and for a moment, he wondered what she was going to do. And what she did next was exactly what he wanted. Her lips were hard against his. He slid his hands around her waist, drawing her closer still, her breasts pushed up against his chest, her hips hard against his, her legs floating around his, as she wrapped her arms around him and the kiss deepened.

The cool water was intensely erotic against his heated skin. His hands moved under her rounded bottom and gripped her tight, as the lively waves struck their bodies. He held her hard against him so that she would know his need intimately.

She let go of him, and for a moment, he wondered if she was going to swim away, but instead, she pulled off her G string and tossed it onto the pontoon and pulled down his shorts. She slid her legs around his hips, pushing onto him with one swift movement.

He started with surprise as her wet heat enveloped him. He thrust into her, but she pushed herself away from him. "I just wanted to feel you… natural for a moment. I assume you have some protection in that picnic basket of yours?"

He nodded. It had been the first thing he'd thought of.

"Good." She grinned. "Then I'm looking forward even more to my picnic… after my swim."

He adjusted his shorts and pushed himself up onto the pontoon, watching her wriggle back into her G string and swim away. It was less of a tease and more of a taster for what was to come. And he couldn't wait.

He'd never known such extreme need, never known himself to be so aroused before. This woman with no home and only one name, with a personality to match his own, seemed to know instinctively how to please him, matching his desire with her own.

She was amazing. And she was an enigma. He felt that the two were probably related. Once he knew her, would she be less amazing? Somehow he doubted it.

She waved and then turned back and swam with a sleek overarm style, plowing through the water, straight past the pontoon, as if he weren't there. Being ignored was strange. He was used to being the center of attention, the center of everyone's orbit. People came to him, and he sent people away from him. That was his life. But this woman's careless attitude toward him only made him want her more. He dived into the water and followed her to shore.

Her bronzed butt was a clear sign that she was accustomed to nude sunbathing. She turned to him with a warm, inviting smile. She extended her hand to him and drew him toward the cliffs' privacy, where no one—not even his security team—could see them. And there she showed him that the tease out at sea was more a promise —a promise she amply fulfilled.

MUCH LATER, after their lust was sated, he opened the hamper and withdrew a bottle of chilled champagne. He poured a couple of glasses and passed one to her. She took a sip and looked around.

"I'll always remember this moment," she murmured, huskily. "The perfect life—champagne, swimming to a reef—even if we couldn't swim on it—sunshine, and a man who would be perfect if he weren't king." Her expression had turned serious, her dark eyes a place you could get lost in.

He frowned. "You don't like the fact I'm king?" He didn't know if he felt irritated or amused by the fact. It was certainly unusual. "Most people seem quite impressed."

She chewed her cheek, the dimple disappearing briefly. "Maybe I'm not most people."

"I can definitely agree with you on that one. What is it that isn't impressive about me?" He sounded needy, which wasn't like him, but he had the uneasy feeling he was entering new territory with Shakira.

She glanced at him and then back at her champagne and then stretched her long legs in front of her. Her lips quirked into a brief smile. "You're good at sex, I'll give you that. And I like you. I really like you. But, no, I'm not impressed by royalty."

Annoyingly reassured, but even more curious than before, he sat beside her and took a sip of his champagne. "You must know other royals, then."

She should have shaken her head or nodded. It was one of those times when a one-word answer would suffice. It would have at least satisfied his curiosity. She did neither. "I'm a basic kind of girl. And I like a man with no ties. And royalty equals ties."

He couldn't argue with that because he liked the same in his women. No ties, no complications. But it galled him for the boot to be on the other foot.

"Then why not, for today, forget that I am king"—he tapped his glass against hers—"and we can simply enjoy ourselves. How long do you intend to stay in Sharq Havilah?"

She tilted her head back, and he noticed her eyes were closed beneath her glasses. "Two days. I'm leaving your country in two days."

"And you're going to…" He let his sentence drift away, hoping she'd supply the ending.

She turned a dimpled grin to him, obviously knowing what he wanted and equally obviously, not about to give it to him. "Away. I'm going away."

It seemed she was determined to retain her air of mystery and tell him nothing about herself. She was the perfect woman for him. It was the kind of relationship he'd always wanted. Then how come it didn't seem enough now?

"Fair enough." It wasn't, but he wasn't about to come over all needy again. He lay back on the hot, abrasive sand beside her. "Then we have just now, just us." He rolled onto his side to face her, twisted the end of a wet strand of her hair and tickled her cheek. She swatted him away but also rolled on her side to face him. They were nearly touching, and he was ready for her once more.

"Sounds good to me."

They laid aside their champagne and wriggled closer. He allowed himself the pleasure of the sensation of her silky skin against his fingertips as they explored each other. Her mind and identity were to remain a mystery, but her body he was determined to know. And he did.

. . .

AFTER THEY HAD MADE LOVE a second time, Shakira rolled onto her back and let the hot sun soak into her limbs. She had spent two years in the English chill until it had seeped into her bones and refused to leave. It had settled deep, alongside the grief over the deaths of her mother and brothers, and distrust of her increasingly erratic remaining brother. Grief, darkness, and distrust—she was sick of them. She basked in the heat of the sun and Roshan's appreciation like a subterranean creature emerging into the light for the first time.

It seemed nothing was ever lukewarm in her life—not least, her feelings for King Roshan of Sharq Havilah. The man she couldn't hate. Because how could she despise a man exactly like her, a man in whom she could lose herself? She couldn't remember the last time she'd lost herself.

And so she gave herself over to the physicality of the afternoon—hot hours of lovemaking, conversations both playful and soulful, and frivolous enjoyment such as she'd never enjoyed before. Such as, she could see, he rarely allowed himself. It wasn't until they'd returned to the palace—his arm casually around her shoulders, as if they were a regular couple—that her phone rang. She froze. Her past had caught up with her, taunting her for having forgotten—even if it were for only an afternoon.

"You go on inside," she said. "I just have to take this call."

He nodded. "I'll wait for you at the entrance. I don't want you to be debarred." He grinned and squeezed her hand, and ran up the steps. She tore her eyes away from his tall, muscled body and, when he was out of earshot, answered the phone.

She turned her face away from the palace and the waiting king. "Yes," she said abruptly. "What do you want?"

"You know what we want," Nabeel said, his voice menacing. She could tell he was high on his drug of choice.

"It's not possible. I can't reach him."

Laughter echoed in her ears. "Oh, I think you can. In fact, I can see him standing quite close to you right at this moment."

She looked around suddenly, searching the perimeter of the palace, and saw a glimpse of a camera lens, shining in the bright afternoon light. "I won't do it," she said fiercely, resolute now she knew who she was dealing with.

"You will. It is your duty, Shakira. Think of your mother. Think of your brothers. You owe your life to them. Do not let them down. Do not let me down. You must get anything—photos, intel of any kind which will further our cause to destabilize our enemies."

The phone went dead in her ear, and she slipped it into her pocket before glaring at the now retreating gleam of the telephoto lens aimed at her. She took a deep breath and then turned to the palace where she could see Roshan talking to someone inside.

He turned to her as if he was somehow aware that she was looking at him and smiled and nodded. Her mother. Her brothers. She had no choice. Besides, what would a few innocent photos matter to Roshan? Nothing. But they'd appease her brother, and if she wished to return to the country she loved, she had no choice.

Her walk turned into a run as she ascended the stairs into the palace.

CHAPTER 4

Shakira wasn't sure when it had happened. But at some point during the twenty-four hours since she'd first set eyes on Roshan, she realized she'd made a connection with this man, quite unlike anything that had gone before. She hadn't meant to do that.

At first, it has been easy to flirt with this handsome and amusing man. It had always been a part of her, which she had purposely suppressed. Apart from her time in Oxford, life had revolved around her family. She'd always been the dutiful daughter, kept out of the limelight until the day a suitable husband could be found for her. Until now.

She watched as Roshan spoke briefly to the maid who was serving them dinner, unable to stop herself from being captivated by his warm manner and consideration. He might be king, he might be all-powerful in his country, but at heart, he was simply a charming man. There was no other word for it. And he had undoubtedly charmed her—

more than she had meant him to. What had started as a harmless bit of fun, had become something much more.

"Am I boring you that much?" asked Roshan with a smile, as he turned back toward her. "You've been quiet all evening."

"Maybe I'm always quiet?" suggested Shakira.

"You're certainly not always quiet." It was his turn to look thoughtful. "Based on my intimate knowledge of you over these past twenty-four hours, that is," he said with a smile.

She took a sip of champagne and met his gaze. She had to snap out of it. He was becoming curious.

"Maybe I've found myself in an unusual situation." A little truth would be believable.

He leaned back in his chair and swilled the effervescent liquid around his glass thoughtfully. "I'm quite glad you're not accustomed to this situation, that you don't go around seducing kings every day."

"Did I seduce you, or did you seduce me?"

"Good point," he said. "I think everything we have done has been by mutual consent, and by mutual desire. Don't you agree?"

"I do agree. In fact, so far, we don't seem to have disagreed on very much."

"They say the strength of the relationship is the sum total of their disagreements."

"Who are they?"

He shrugged. "You know, the they who know everything. I think they may have a point in this case. Perhaps we should try it out? Now, what do people tend to disagree about most? Sex? I think we pretty much agree on that one. Religion? You are of the same faith as me, I think. Which brings me to the next big one—politics."

She took a big gulp of her champagne. He noticed.

"Politics," he repeated.

"Probably not relevant in our situation."

He raised an eyebrow. "You think so?"

She shrugged. "Unless I am about to stage a coup, or run for office, or marry you"—she ignored his splutter—"I hardly think it relevant."

"Okay," he said slowly, putting down his glass on the mahogany table. "I think we can safely say you don't intend to topple my kingdom. So we'll pass over politics. Tell me, what would you like to talk about?"

It was a good question because the choices were limited. But there was one obvious thing they both wanted. She rose from the table, the chair scraping on the tiled floor. "You know, I think talk is over-rated. I agree with the adage that actions speaks louder than words."

She had his attention now. She swept her hands down the satin gown, smoothing its wrinkles, and walked around the edge of the table and stood beside him. He didn't move. He appeared content to see what she would do. He had learned that much about her—she was a person of action, often unpredictable.

She stood a little apart from him and extended her hand. He didn't take his eyes off hers. As he took her hand she gave it a little tug, and he rose. She liked the way he was taller than her—much taller.

"I'd like to dance."

The tension left his face, and he smiled. "That, my lady, can be arranged."

She turned towards the music center she'd seen earlier

in the corner of the room, but he stopped her from moving.

"If you'd like to dance, Shakira, we will do it properly."

It seemed he'd always get his way. She might begin something, but he would take it in an entirely different direction. Usually, she liked to take control, but there was something profoundly thrilling and exciting about allowing him to.

Hand-in-hand they walked out of the dining room and into the public area of the palace—empty now that the majority of workers had left the building. He opened the door of the state ballroom. He took a taper and lit the candles which were placed around the wall in sconces. Little by little, the place was lent a beauty that it didn't have in the daylight.

He left the room for a moment and then returned. A few moments later, a couple of musicians entered and began a waltz.

She laughed. "Do you have musicians on standby, just in case they're needed?"

"I happened to know they were rehearsing for a concert in one of the palace rooms."

"I think I'm a little disappointed," she teased, as she accepted his outstretched hand.

"Then I'll always make sure to have musicians available in case I need them. Twenty-four hours a day."

She laughed as she was swept along, guided by his hand on the small of her back, the other gripping her free hand, and they swept around the room in time to the music. It should have been incongruous, it should have been strange, but being led by him in graceful movements, their bodies, as usual, in sync, felt so right.

They continued to dance as one piece of music led into another until the candles began to sputter, and the music faded. He pulled her into his arms in the center of the room beneath the glittering chandelier, lit only by the reflected lights of the candles along the wall.

"I don't know about you," he whispered. "But I think I'm ready for bed."

She had to agree. Dancing with limited contact, gazing into his eyes, had raised her desire to a pitch that needed to be satisfied. She nodded.

He dismissed the musicians, took her hand, in the same manner that he had held it during the waltz, and they swept out of the ballroom. It wasn't far along the corridors to his suite of rooms.

As soon as they entered his room, they were in each other's arms. The beautiful red satin dress he'd had ordered for her that afternoon fell into in a pool at her feet as he swept her into his arms and his bed.

There was something different about the lovemaking now. Both of them were taking their time, appreciating each other's bodies in a way they hadn't the other times they'd been intimate. It partly came from a subdued feeling she'd had ever since her brother's phone call, and partly from Roshan.

He was tender as if she'd somehow got behind his defenses, as he'd got behind hers. She was getting in too deep. She realized that, as he penetrated her and sent her into a cloud of satisfaction and sensory explosion. As she emerged from the sensations, and night settled around them, she thought again that, not only was she getting in too deep, but she was in danger of getting out of her depth. But her last thought as she drifted into a sleep brought on by complete, sensate exhaustion, was she didn't think she cared.

As the day turned into morning and they rose leisurely, it seemed Roshan had postponed much of his work, much to the chagrin of his advisors. He turned to her as he ushered yet another official out of his office. They kept glancing at her uneasily. And well they might, she thought.

She rose and kissed him. "Your officials don't seem especially pleased by my presence."

"That's an understatement. But a few days of pleasure is hardly a lot to ask when I'll be working the rest of the time."

"After I'm gone," she said, with a brief smile before walking past him and picking up a folder in a desultory fashion. She dropped it again and glanced at his open computer. She turned to find him frowning as he watched her.

"You're still leaving the day after tomorrow?"

"I am," she said. She'd have to. She had no other choice. Besides, she knew that, at some point, he wouldn't want her around. They both had very different lives to lead.

"And you're still not telling me where you're going to?"

"Why would you want to know? You're hardly going to be following me, are you?" She picked something up and replaced it. She felt nervous, edgy even. She crossed her arms over her crisp white linen shirt and rested against his desk. "You have your agenda to follow."

"Does that mean that you have an agenda, too?" he asked. He was too acute. Too smart.

She pushed herself from the table and slipped her fingers around the nape of his neck, and kissed him. "Doesn't everyone?" When cornered, deflect the enemy with whatever weapon you have. She blinked as she reflected on her thoughts. Did she see him as the enemy? Was she using sex as a weapon?

As usual, he took her action and twisted it, holding her tight against him. He kissed her more thoroughly, making her forget her thoughts and any agenda items, too. He pulled away far too soon and glanced at the clock. "We have to get going."

"Ah, yes," she said. "We have a wedding to attend. But one at which I'm to remain hidden, behind the scenes."

He didn't return her smile. "You know the score, Shakira." He swept his thumb over her swollen lips. "It's down to me. I have to marry, and we must be discrete."

She nodded. She knew the score. Probably better than him.

Roshan glanced around Zavian and Gabrielle's wedding reception until he saw who he was looking for. Shakira was doing exactly as he'd asked. She was wearing a—for her—demure outfit whose effect was anything but demure, and talking casually to someone at the bottom end of the table. He'd arranged it behind his friends Zavian's and Amir's backs. They need not know —and to all intents and purposes, Shakira was simply a friend of a friend of Gabrielle's, assigned to a place at the lower end of the room. Their gazes snagged briefly, and for a moment he was caught, like a fly in a trap. He'd fallen for her bad. He tugged his gaze away, feeling angry at being trapped—not by Shakira—but by circumstances. He turned his attention back to the other two kings.

"You certainly didn't waste any time," said Roshan, taking a sip of his champagne. He indicated Zavian's advisor. "I bet the old man wasn't impressed with only having a month to organize the wedding."

Zavian smiled. "Indeed. But he didn't make a fuss. I think he was relieved I was getting married at all."

"That anyone would have you," added Amir, with a smile.

Zavian's gaze rested on Gabrielle, who was talking with Ruby and Hani—Amir's wife and son. "She nearly didn't," he commented.

"No," said Roshan. "She's far too clever to consider a wealthy, powerful king to be a good match."

Zavian ignored his comment. No doubt realizing that Roshan, despite his sarcastic tone, actually meant it. Roshan didn't consider kings to be a good match. Particularly in recent times. He chanced another glance at Shakira. He couldn't help thinking that if he weren't king, he and Shakira could have a future together. Not for the first time, Roshan hated not only his position in life, but also himself. If he were stronger, less dutiful, he'd do something about it.

"You're right. It had to be love," said Zavian. "And, as it happened. I'm madly in love with her."

Roshan watched as Zavian looked at his new wife, Gabrielle, who positively glowed in the soft lights. Love shone in his expression, as did a far more earthy lust. Now lust, Roshan recognized more easily.

Roshan groaned. "For goodness sake, take her to bed,

now, and be done with it." He shook his head, and Amir laughed.

Amir clapped his hand on Roshan's back and addressed Zavian. "Our friend Roshan is a cynic, Zavian."

Reluctantly, Zavian withdrew his gaze from Gabrielle, who was making her way over to him. "Yes, but not for long. The Tawazun princess is beautiful, and you've always appreciated a beautiful woman, Roshan. Maybe the appreciation will develop into love." Zavian looked over Roshan's shoulder.

Roshan shrugged and glanced back toward where he'd last seen Shakira, but she'd disappeared. He couldn't be bothered to answer. He didn't know whether it was Zavian and Amir's evident happiness, which underlined his own dismal future prospects—prospects which he hadn't been bothered about until he'd met Shakira. But whatever, he felt a shadow over himself, which he was having a hard time removing. Amir and Zavian had picked up on his mood, and he knew they were both wondering what was eating him. But he didn't have the interest to satisfy their concerns. They'd both passed the buck—in the form of the sheikha—to him, and he was landed with it. He wasn't feeling exactly kindly toward either of them.

Then Zavian pulled Gabrielle into his arms and kissed her—their love apparent for all to see—not caring that the whole room watched them. It was the last straw.

Amir nodded over Roshan's shoulder. "Talking of the sheikha, it looks like she's coming over to talk to you."

Roshan felt a sinking in his belly, not because Sheikha Elaheh of Tawazun was an awful woman—quite the contrary, she was beautiful, intelligent, if not a little scary.

He hardly knew her. Whenever she was with her family, she was watched over by her eagle-eyed father.

He turned to see her coming towards him. He had to admit she was beautiful in an elegant kind of way. He couldn't help comparing the sheikha's sharp bone structure and almost military bearing—she kept her shoulders well back, and her head held high—to the lush curves of Shakira. Talking of whom. He glanced around but couldn't see her. Good. He didn't particularly want Shakira to see him with the sheikha, or vice versa. It would be like two worlds colliding, which he'd much prefer to keep separate.

"Roshan," Elaheh said with a small inclination of her beautiful face, hair severely pulled back to reveal eyes glittering and intense. She extended a bejeweled hand, and he kissed it. At that moment, he felt a prickle down his spine. He straightened up quickly and looked around to find himself staring into Shakira's face, a hurt look clearly visible in her eyes.

It seems separate was too much to be hoped for. He was glad the other kings were out of sight.

He turned back to the sheikha. "Elaheh."

Elaheh looked from him to Shakira. "Aren't you going to introduce us, Roshan?"

Heat prickled at his neck. He'd always kept up his guard and had managed never to be caught out before, never torn between duty and his amorous adventures. It seemed his luck had just run out.

He smiled, hoping the fixed grin would hide the unexpected tumult of emotions that filled him. "Of course, Elaheh." He looked at Shakira and nearly lost the smile as her eyes held his steadily. "This is my friend, Shakira."

Whatever the criticisms he'd heard about Elaheh, he had to admit that she was gracious on such an occasion.

She held out her hand to Shakira, and after only a moment's hesitation, Shakira took it, and they gripped each other for longer than was usual.

"It's a pleasure to meet you, Shakira," said Elaheh. "I had not expected you to be here."

Roshan was momentarily puzzled. "Do you two know each other?"

Elaheh released Shakira's hand and shifted her arrogant gaze to him. "I only know of her, Roshan. She has been your..." She paused, he suspected, for dramatic effect. It worked. "Your most *recent* friend."

He cleared his throat uncomfortably and glanced at Shakira, who didn't look in the least put-out. In fact, she had a smile on her lips, which surprised him.

"You're correct, Princess," said Shakira. "And I apologize if my presence here is unwelcome to you."

"Not at all," said Elaheh unconvincingly. "Roshan and I have a business arrangement, which I'm sure you won't interfere with. Will you?"

"No, indeed. I assure you that our... friendship will be as transitory as Roshan's other friendships."

"Ah, good." For the first time, Roshan saw Elaheh smile. "I see we understand each other." Elaheh beckoned for a waiter to bring over some drinks and offered one to Shakira. "Come, take a drink with me."

Roshan's heart sank a little further, and he followed behind the two women—one to whom he was about to become engaged, the other, his lover. Life could be difficult sometimes. But the only alternative was to leave them alone, and then he wouldn't know what was being said. He had no choice but to stay with them.

Shakira shot him an amused glance. "Of course."

They seated themselves at a discreetly placed table and chairs. He leaned against a wall and watched them. It seemed they didn't mind him close, but he wasn't required for the conversation. He wondered what Elaheh was up to.

"You look familiar, Shakira. Have we met before?"

Shakira glanced up quickly at Roshan, and he frowned, interested to hear her response.

She shook her head. "I don't believe so. I've been in England, studying at Oxford, the past few months, but have returned to visit family."

Elaheh took a leisurely sip of her sparking juice, placing her glass delicately on the table before sitting back and looking at Shakira. She didn't answer immediately. He didn't know about Shakira, but even he was unnerved by Elaheh's steely, uncompromising gaze.

"And where is your home? The color of your skin and eyes suggest you are of our people, and yet you have blonde hair."

Shakira swallowed and glanced around as if trying to find an escape. She obviously decided there was none, however.

"Danish. My mother was Danish. She came to… my homeland and fell in love with my father. My siblings are dark. I am the only one to inherit her coloring. I'd have preferred it if I hadn't."

"Really? And why is that? I imagine the men love it. A change from their dark-haired womenfolk."

Shakira shrugged. "Maybe. But it makes me feel like an outsider in my own home."

"Ah, you mention 'home' for the first time. And where is that?"

Shakira locked eyes with Elaheh and opened her mouth to speak but checked herself and closed her mouth again with a smile and shake of the head. "I can't tell you, I'm afraid."

Elaheh cocked her head to one side. "Can't? That's strange. Is there a reason?"

While Roshan was also interested in the answer to Elaheh's question, he couldn't resist Shakira's appealing glance at him. Her eyes begged him for help. He came and stood above them both, hands in pockets, looking from one to the other with a polite smile. As if, for all the world, he was politely chatting to acquaintances at a cocktail party.

"Maybe because she doesn't have to, Elaheh? Or maybe because this isn't an inquisition. Shakira is here as my guest, and I'd prefer if you didn't interrogate her."

Shakira frowned and blinked, as if not liking his response. Elaheh rose and gave him an icy stare. "We are to be married, Roshan. I'll let your paramour go for now, but I will have final say on such things in the future."

She walked off, elegant and upright. He suddenly realized that the woman he was about to marry wasn't the subservient, obedient daughter of their ally, which the three kings had always assumed. The King of Tawazun had always hidden her character, and now he was beginning to see why. The Sheikha of Tawazun was a formidable woman.

He looked back at Shakira, who shook her head, looked upset, and walked away quickly.

"Shakira!" He tried to hold onto her arm as she walked past, but she shook it off with a small cry.

He followed her outside, not caring to stay in the company of his friends, the kings, or any other people his life revolved around. Their three countries had always been close, and this wedding had brought them all together. But now, for the first time, he felt alienated from his world. Something had shifted since he'd met Shakira, and he needed to be with her. She was upset, and therefore so was he. It was as if they were in tune. It didn't bode well for an easy future.

He stepped out into the fresh air of the garden and looked around. It was only on the second scan that he saw her. Her white dress was almost fluorescent under the moonlight, briefly catching his vision.

He thrust his hands in his pockets as he tried to wrestle with the tumult of emotions that ran through his brain. He should stop this craziness. He was destined for another, but he could no more walk away from Shakira than from his own shadow. Their minds were as one with everything, and their bodies? They were joined at every opportunity. He couldn't get enough of her. And the thought scared him.

"Shakira," he said softly. "Are you all right?"

She wiped her hand across her eyes, smudging her make-up. She nodded, but he wasn't convinced. He looked around and saw something move in the corner of his eye. Zavian's glance passed over him with a shrug as he and Gabrielle walked through the courtyard. He and Shakira had been seen together. Roshan regretted it, but he'd hardly hidden Shakira very well. He should have known he wouldn't be able to see her without touching her.

He pushed Zavian to the back of his mind. He'd explain—as best he could—to Zavian and Amir later. But now, all he had on his mind was the woman in front of him, whose eyes showed a distress he was desperate and utterly unable to ease.

"You're not, I see that," he said with a sigh. "You knew she'd be here. You knew we are to be engaged."

She swallowed and nodded. "I knew, but it's different seeing her face to face. I think we should go. This is too public. She might see us again, and…" She trailed off.

"And you don't want that."

She shook her head. "And nor should you. She's a smart woman who doesn't deserve to be used as she is. By her father, or by you, or me."

"As you say, she's smart. She knows what she's getting into."

"Are you sure about that? Do any of us?"

There was laughter from the path, and more people walked past, throwing them curious glances. He frowned. He moved her hair off her face to see her better, revealing the extent of her discomfort and anxiety.

"You're right. Let's get out of here."

He put his arm around her, and they walked through the shadowy paths, avoiding the main route to the exit, and made their way to their guest quarters. At least here, he thought, they could be their true selves. But it was not to be. When he reached his suite, he found his phone and emails were full of requests, and one of his staff was waiting to see him. Something was going on.

"Wait in the bedroom. I won't be long. It looks like something has come up, which I need to deal with." He walked to the adjoining office and shut the door.

"So, what's so important that you come to me at midnight, Hasan?" he asked his assistant.

SHAKIRA PACED THE FLOOR. Meeting Elaheh had somehow shifted all the pieces back into focus. She hated that she might have hurt Elaheh, and she hated how Elaheh must have seen her, must have imagined her to be—the other woman.

She couldn't continue this charade any longer. Each moment she was with Roshan, she sank further under his spell. She was getting in too deep, and she could see that he was, too. At first, she'd imagined that a flirtation with the Playboy King would go no further. But there were moments, now, when she could see in his eyes, and the things he nearly said, that he was feeling the same deep attraction to her, that she felt to him.

She couldn't do it to him. When it had been nothing but pure sexual fun, it had been okay. But now? She couldn't use him like that. She wasn't that person. She'd ignore her brother and risk the consequences.

She pivoted on the balls of her feet, her dress falling around her, and crossed her arms. She'd have this last night, and then she'd leave. Disappear. She looked through at the closed door behind which Roshan was working. She owed him that much. He'd given her pleasure of which she'd only dreamed, and he'd opened her eyes to the hatred which had ruled her whole life, exposing its stupidity. She'd loved with him, and she'd learned much from him. She owed him alright.

The door opened, and he came through. He pushed his hair from his face and gave her a worried smile. She frowned. He looked tired and anxious.

"Everything sorted?" she asked.

He shrugged. "It will be in the morning. It's probably nothing."

She smoothed his hair and slid the palm of her hand around his cheek. He held it close and kissed her palm. A shiver ran through her body and lingered inside her. "So…" She smiled at the prospect of what lay ahead. "To bed?"

He put his arms around her and slipped down the shoestring straps of her dress and kissed the top of her breasts. "You read my mind."

And to bed they went. And she allowed herself that night to be entirely his woman. Because she knew it would be the last.

CHAPTER 5

The next morning when Roshan awoke, he knew the bed was empty because he felt empty. He opened one eye at the sound of feet walking across the floor and reached out and grabbed her hand. She squealed in surprise as he pulled her to him, and she fell on top of him.

As his hands swept down her body, he frowned. "You're fully dressed."

The light instantly faded from her face as if she'd remembered something. She pressed her lips together with a rueful grimace and stood up. "I told you I was leaving."

"You did, indeed, but I assumed we'd be returning to Sharq Havilah together, and you'd leave from there."

She shrugged and turned her back to him to finish off her makeup. "It's just as easy to fly to Dubai from here," she said, widening her eyes in the mirror and applying mascara. He watched, entranced, as she blinked in the mirror to assess the results. While her long lashes needed no makeup to make her large eyes beautiful, the addition of mascara took her eyes from beautiful to stunning in a few deft applications. They were eyes whose beauty would never fade with the passing of the years.

He frowned as he realized that, for the first time, he'd imagined the woman he was with growing older alongside him. Ridiculous! Or was it? What if Sheikha Elaheh of Tawazun decided to marry someone else? What if he were free to choose his wife? What then? That was a whole lot of "what-ifs", but he couldn't help adding yet another one. What if he made sure he didn't lose touch with Shakira? He was king and had the means to make sure he didn't, after all.

"You're staying in Dubai, then?"

She gave an ambiguous grunt, selecting a lipstick from her makeup purse, and stretched out her lips in the mirror. She swept the blood-red lipstick across first her top lip and then the lower. She had beautiful full lips. He sighed and propped himself up on his elbow to better observe her. He thought he could do this all day—simply watch her. He didn't ever remember thinking that before. Usually, he was impatient for his lovers to leave so he could get on with life. But now he realized he wanted Shakira beside him as he got on with life. It wouldn't be easy, that was for sure.

"Shakira," he said softly. "I need to know how to contact you."

She looked up and met his gaze in the mirror. He frowned at her expression. How could she be fearful because he wanted to contact her? There was something awkward about her movements now, a self-consciousness which was at odds with the woman he was getting to know.

She dabbed at her lips with the lipstick before pressing them together. The effect was spectacular. "You knew what you were getting into, Roshan. You're to be married, and I don't see how contacting me will be a good idea."

He was beginning to feel irritated now. The roles had reversed, and she was saying the kind of things he'd always told his lovers. There was nothing for it. He had to resort to the pressure he knew she'd have difficulty withstanding.

"Come here," he softly growled.

She shook her head stiffly and refused to meet his gaze in the mirror.

"You dare to refuse your king's command?" he growled.

"You're not my king," she said, before blushing prettily.

"Then who is?"

She shook her head and tried to fit her earring into her pierced ear without success. She swore under her breath as she tried again.

He jumped out of bed, took the earring from her hands, and gently fixed it in place. They were close, but her eyes were lowered. He brushed her cheek with his forefinger. "There you are."

She turned back to face the mirror, and he placed his hands on her shoulders and looked at her reflection. She dabbed her lipstick on her bottom lip, which distracted him from his original question. He cast his mind back to the magic they could create and sighed.

"You have beautiful lips. Have I told you that?"

"Yes." She smiled before slotting the lipstick back into

the case. She turned around and tried to step past him, but it seemed she was also easily distracted as her gaze raked his hips and chest, and his body responded accordingly. She shook her head and brought her ruby red lips to his and softly kissed him, playing with the tip of his tongue against hers.

He groaned and put his arms around her and kissed her harder. He felt her soften in his arms, and when they eventually parted, she plucked a tissue and ran it over his lips, wiping off the lipstick with a smile. She tried to turn away, but he held her closer, his hands moving around and under her breasts, lifting them so he could kiss their tops, pushing down her shirt to expose her bra. One flick and it was undone, and her full breasts spilled into his waiting hands and hungry mouth.

He felt her control slip as her breathing quickened. When he glanced up, her eyes were closed, and she caught her breath as her arousal increased. He knew what she liked, now, and knew that she could climax simply by him playing with her breasts. He didn't want that now, though. He was hungry for more.

He slid his hands under her bottom and lifted her hard against him. Her legs slid into place around his hips, and he carried her back to the bed.

"Do you know what I'm going to do to you?"

"Surprise me," she murmured, her lids half-closed. "I like surprises." She licked her smiling lips.

He lifted her dress, peeled off her panties, opened her legs wide, and settled himself between them. His hands caressed her thighs and hips, his mouth and tongue exploring her wet sex, lathing her until she exploded in a noisy climax, gripping his head and shouting his name.

He drew back with a smile, drinking her in. She was a goddess—a sexual goddess.

It was only when she fell back on the pillow, one hand hooked behind her head that their gaze snagged and caught and stayed. And, at that moment, he knew that nothing would be the same again. His sexual goddess had become something much more to him. And he hadn't even seen it coming.

SHAKIRA HADN'T MEANT to return to bed with Roshan. She'd intended to have been dressed and ready to leave before he'd awoken. Only then would she be safe from him. As soon as he looked at her with that wicked gaze, as soon as she felt his touch upon her body, his lips upon hers, she was gone.

But this time it was different. Something had been slowly changing in their lovemaking. The only word she could think of to describe how he touched her, how he eased himself into her, the way in which his eyes caressed her was... Her thoughts stuttered over the word. But there was only one word to describe it. Loving.

She shook her head. Ridiculous. His life was about to take another turn, and so, most definitely, was hers. Yes, she'd return to her home, but she couldn't allow herself to be controlled by her brother anymore. Her brief time with Roshan showed her that she wanted no part of her brother's plans to make their country great by continuing the hatred and attacks against the three countries that comprised Havilah. When she returned to Jazira—her homeland and long-time enemy of Havilah—she'd work to find a better way forward.

And while she smoothed away the damage that their lovemaking had done to her hair and makeup and adjusted her clothing, she listened to the shower stop. She sat and waited for Roshan to emerge because she knew she couldn't leave without saying goodbye. Not now.

She jumped as Roshan's phone pinged suddenly beside her. Automatically, she looked at the screen and felt a sinking sensation in her stomach. It was a message from the sheikha of Tawazun, Elaheh. Behind it, she saw that the photo Roshan had taken of her that first night they'd been together. He was using it as the phone's background. Her heart chilled. If her brother ever saw this image he'd know she'd failed in her mission; she looked too happy. She only paused a moment before trying a few obvious codes to enter Roshan's phone, determined to delete the photo. But, before she could achieve her aim, Roshan entered the room, a towel slung low around his hips while he dried his hair with another towel.

"Was that my phone?"

She nodded, and quickly switched off the phone. "Sheikha Elaheh," she said without thinking. "I… happened to see the screen." She shrugged. "Force of habit to pick up the phone. I'm sorry. I didn't mean to pry." She felt fidgety and ill-at-ease at what she was about to do.

He frowned slightly and took the phone from her hands, entered his code and checked the message. He tossed the phone down. "It's okay. She just wants to meet up later."

"Feel free to contact her."

"She can wait." He glanced at her and turned away too quickly, as if not liking what he saw. "You're still leaving then."

"Of course." She cleared her throat. She had to be strong. "Did you really think sex would change my mind?"

"Sex," he repeated. He turned slowly to her. "You know? I think I did."

She had no choice, she reminded herself. She had to leave because when he found out who she was, he'd hate her and she couldn't bear to be around when that happened.

"I'm still leaving."

"Just like that?"

"Just like that." She tried a smile. It didn't quite reach her eyes, but it was better than nothing. "We had fun, didn't we?"

"We did." He finished drying his hair and tossed the towel to one side, leaned against the desk and folded his arms. "And, no doubt, we'll see each other around."

"No doubt," she repeated, too long after him.

"No doubt," he repeated, his hands on his hips as he faced her. He narrowed his eyes. "Say it again, like you mean it."

She clamped her hand on her bag like a weapon. "We always knew it wasn't going to last. You're to be married soon, as am I."

"They are arranged marriages. Our affair will hurt no one. Certainly not my intended. Come on, you're creating problems where there are none."

"There *are* problems, believe me."

"I don't."

"Then…" She hesitated. "We'll have to agree to disagree."

He shook his head. "You don't have to go, Shakira."

"Ah, but I do. And," she said, rising to her feet and dropping her phone in her bag, "I think this is all about the fact you're annoyed that I'm leaving you. I doubt you're used to it." She sighed, in an exaggerated, 'you're making a fuss of something simple' kind of way. "Look, if we meet up again, that would be nice, more than nice." He wasn't to know that if they ever did meet up again, there was no way he'd want to spend any time with her. "But, for now, I have to leave. I'm just getting on my with life. It's no big deal."

He didn't answer but gave her a sensual, knowing smile. She frowned briefly, wondering what he was thinking, whether he believed he could keep her here against her wishes. But she knew, deep down, that he'd never do that.

"Goodbye then," she said. This time she didn't wait for an answer but quickly slipped through the door and closed it without a backward glance.

She was doing the right thing, she told herself as she walked quickly through the palace to the waiting taxi. Their relationship had no future. He might not know it yet, but he would. She stopped dead in her tracks as the realization that she'd most probably never see him again hit her with the force of a truck. She stood for a moment to blink back the tears. She swiped at her cheek with the back of her hand and continued on her way.

ROSHAN WATCHED her stop briefly before continuing through the courtyard to wipe something from her eye before she disappeared through the double doors which led to the side entrance. She had a taxi waiting. He knew that. He also knew that it was taking her to the airport. Now he knew which flight she would be on.

But if she thought this was goodbye, she was wrong. He knew what she felt because it was clear in her eyes, and in how she reacted to his touch. He knew that she didn't want this to end, that she thought she was doing the right thing.

She didn't think he was serious, but he'd show her just how serious he was. He might have a marriage looming, but love wasn't involved with this marriage—it was purely political.

He smiled to himself as he watched her go. She was putting on a front. He knew it had been more than fun to her, just as it had been to him. And he'd show her how much she meant to him later.

He'd surprise her. He knew how much she enjoyed surprises.

But for now, he needed to focus on business. He tossed his phone in the air, caught it, and tapped Elaheh's name. No doubt she wanted to progress the marriage talks, and he had no objection to that. He and Elaheh were the same —they both knew the deal. And he'd make sure Shakira did, too.

"YOU WANTED TO SEE ME, PRINCESS," said Roshan, smiling at the beautiful woman who sat among her advisors like a queen bee amid a hive of workers. She was beautiful and smart but also terrifying. He could never love her, but he could marry her. After all, it would mean nothing to either of them, would it? For the first time, he felt a flutter of doubt, which he quickly ignored.

"Yes, Your Highness." She beckoned him impatiently forward. "But perhaps we can dispense with the formality. We both know each other's names."

He managed to smother the laugh which rose unbidden in surprise at her words. He hardly knew her, but each time he saw her, she surprised him further. "Of course, whatever you prefer."

She indicated a seat opposite her. He glanced at its location, with the full blast of the sun coming down on it. It was usual for a king to have the light behind him. But it seemed that Princess Elaheh wasn't interested in putting him at ease. He suspected the opposite.

He sat where indicated. "What can I do for you?"

She rose a haughty eyebrow. "I rather suspect it's the other way around." She waved away her advisors who instantly vanished without demur, obviously accustomed to doing exactly what their decisive princess wished.

Roshan grunted in surprise. "Sounds interesting. And, Princess"—she glared at him—"Elaheh," he corrected. "How do you think I need help?"

"Because you are ignorant of something you should be aware of."

He tilted his head, suddenly alert. "I doubt I am ignorant of anything important. I have my advisors, and we have our spies—" He was stopped mid-sentence by a dismissive wave of her hand.

"Yes, yes." She rolled her eyes. "You are the all-powerful king who is invincible."

He was beginning to feel rattled by her outspokenness.

"I don't regard myself as invincible, but my advisors are proficient at their jobs."

"Is that right?" she said shortly.

"Yes, it is."

She shrugged and rose. "If you're not interested in what I have to say, you may as well leave."

Why was talking to his betrothed like wrestling with a piranha or a snake, or both? "I didn't say I'm not interested, I was merely—"

She cut him short again with an imperious wave of her hand. That would have to stop. He couldn't countenance her impatient gestures after they married. "You were merely being a man. And blind because of it." She sighed and shook her head. "You can have as many advisors as you like, Roshan, but if they're all male and all blind, then it makes no difference."

The blood pounded in Roshan's head. After everything he'd been through with Shakira, all he wanted to do was to follow her and make her see that they could be together. This woman, this princess, who was to be his bride, was driving him crazy. "Just tell me," he exploded, "what it is you want to say!"

Elaheh nodded curtly. "I will. She's a spy."

He opened his eyes wide and poked his head forward, unable to understand what she was saying.

Elaheh grunted. "Don't just sit there with your mouth open. You must do something about it! Imprison her. Find out what she knows about you, your country, and your defenses."

But his mouth refused to close. He shook his head in confusion.

"Do I have to spell it out?" she asked.

He nodded. "Yes, I do believe you do."

"Shakira is a spy."

It didn't help. His mouth simply opened further before he grunted with laughter. "For a moment there, I thought you said Shakira is a spy." He shook his head at the incongruous words. "As if that could happen."

"It could, and it has. Shakira—or to give her full name, Sheikha Shakira of Jazira—came to your country, to your masquerade ball, to you to be precise, to spy for her country."

He spluttered in confusion. "You're trying to tell me that Shakira—my Shakira—" he couldn't stop himself from using the possessive pronoun—"is a spy?" He shook his head. "That's laughable. Have you gone crazy?"

But she wasn't laughing and she didn't look in the least bit crazy. "No, on both counts. I thought she looked familiar when I first saw her. It's a wonder none of you Kings of Havilah recognized the similarity between her and the late Queen of Jazira." She shrugged. "Of course the princess has been kept out of the public eye, and few people know what she looks like. But Shakira is the spitting image of the Queen of Jazira. And when she told me she'd been studying at Oxford, I followed it up. The King of Jazira's sister has been, until recently, studying at Oxford."

"That proves nothing!" Roshan exploded.

"Maybe not," said Elaheh, turning to her right and picking up some papers. "But this does."

He glared at her, unable to countenance any shred of truth in her accusations. He plucked the papers from her hands. And then he saw them. Photographs of him in the garden. Of his laptop in the background. He suddenly remembered how she'd been looking at it.

"I instructed my people to look into her phone records. There were photos of you, the gardens, your innermost private sanctuary, no doubt already in the hands of our enemy—her brother."

A kaleidoscope of images filtered through his mind: of Shakira looking up guiltily from his laptop, of her poring over his phone, taking photos with her own phone. And, most of all, of her reluctance to tell him anything about herself. It was like looking at a checklist, and he could do nothing but tick all the checkboxes, and come up with the same verdict as Elaheh.

Elaheh moved around until she was opposite him, her almond-shaped eyes fixed on his. "Face it, Roshan. You've been well and truly had. Shakira has stitched you up."

He stared at her, unable to contradict her because she was right. Shakira had taken him for a ride right from the first moment they'd met. She'd seduced him, spied on him, and given his and his country's innermost secrets to their enemy—her brother.

"So what are you going to do?" pressed Elaheh.

He shook his head and walked out the door in a daze without answering her. Because there was no way he could tell Elaheh what he planned to do with Shakira if he ever caught up with her again. And none of the things which now played through his mind were the same as they had been only ten minutes earlier.

~

As ROSHAN LOOKED out at the entrance to the airport, sheltered by the car's black-tinted windows, only one thought filled his mind.

Sheikha Elaheh had to be wrong.

Even though intel confirmed Shakira's identity, he still wanted a miracle to happen and for Shakira to be innocent of the crimes of which she stood accused.

The security breach in his own country had been traced to people from Jazira. At first, he hadn't been able to understand what they could hope to do with the information they'd retrieved. It could only be useful if paired with information that was only available on his computer. And not even his assistants had access to that in his rooms.

But after speaking to Elaheh, he'd suddenly remembered finding Shakira looking at his computer, and he'd remembered something she said. He'd remembered the words she'd used to describe her family and her past. It was like the shunting of pieces of a puzzle into place, forming a coherent picture that had been missing. Pieces that had seemed out of place at the time and which had preyed on his mind, suddenly made sense.

All evidence pointed to Shakira being a member of the royal family of Jazira and spying on his country. But still, he couldn't reconcile the woman he'd come to know with this other, damning version of her.

"There she is, Your Majesty," said his security man, who sat next to his chauffeur. The man had his hand on the door. "Shall I get her?"

Elaheh and all the evidence against Shakira had to be wrong.

"No, not yet. We'll follow her. See where she's going."

See if she'll incriminate herself, Roshan thought, because he couldn't believe Shakira was a spy, despite all the evidence to the contrary.

His men shot him puzzled looks but sat back and waited for Roshan's command. They watched her get into a taxi, and Roshan's car purred into life and followed her out of the airport concourse.

They weren't in Dubai. He'd had her on-flights checked and had known her ultimate airport destination now. She had circled back to the opposite side of the gulf to his country. There was an island between the two lands —Jazira. He needed to see, with his own eyes, that this was her ultimate destination.

He didn't have long to wait. As they pulled up a little distance from her, they saw her exit the car, and the taxi driver follow her with her luggage toward the port gates. He held his breath as she walked past the main gates which led to other islands in the gulf and go to the far one, where there was a luxurious speed boat waiting, proudly flying the flag of Jazira. He gritted his teeth.

"Now," he said. "Bring her to me now!"

His security man spoke into his microphone, and men from cars which had been stationed further along the quay leaped into action. Within seconds Shakira was surrounded, before the people on the motorboat could see her.

Roshan approached her, and she jerked her head around to him in surprise. "Roshan!" She swallowed and tried to cover the panic in her eyes. "What are you doing here?"

"I know how much you like surprises, Shakira. So I thought I'd change your plans for you."

She shook her head and shot a look toward the wall behind which her motorboat awaited. "No, I can't."

It was all he needed to hear to confirm his worst fears. "I think you can," he said, his voice low and menacing.

She opened her mouth to speak but instead looked at the burly men who surrounded her, and her attitude changed. She became still and steely. "You would turn your men on me, and force me to come with you?"

"If I have to, yes. Because that, Shakira, is what we do with spies. We imprison them, and we interrogate them, and then we punish them."

He had to hand it to her, he barely saw a flicker of fear in her eyes. Instead, there was something like sadness. He refused to allow it to affect him.

"How did you find out?"

"It doesn't matter. What does matter is that you come with me, now, back to Sharq Havilah to answer some questions."

She took one last look in the direction of the boat. Part of him wanted her to scream, to bring attention to them so she could escape. She could have done it. She was close enough to the boat upon which, undoubtedly, members of the Jazira security force were awaiting her arrival. Maybe that was his rationale for arresting her at the docks—to give her a chance to escape. But, for whatever reason, she didn't. Instead, she pushed aside the guards and walked up to him.

"I think I half-expected it anyway. Let's go."

He signaled for her to get into a waiting car and closed the door on her himself. It was as if something had frozen inside him. He felt cold and hard.

She looked up and wound down the window. "Are you not coming?"

"Yes, but I'm not traveling with you. You are an enemy to me and my country. I will see you back in Sharq Havilah when you are interrogated. When I can find out exactly how and why you traded your body for information."

She gasped and tore her gaze off him and looked straight ahead, her beautiful face a mask, just like his own, just as they'd been when they first met.

His words were hard, but then so was his heart now. It had briefly been softened by her loving, unearthed from the years of darkness since the murder of his parents at the hands of Jaziran mercenaries, but now, like the touch of an icy finger it had instantly hardened to the world once more.

It was easier that way because he could never forgive her for what she'd done—to him and his country. She was his enemy and now would always be.

CHAPTER 6

Shakira paced the small room, back and forward, her feet pounding in time to the pulse in her head. How dare he? She walked up to the locked window and looked out, and thumped her hand against it. How dare he hold her here against her will? She'd been kept here all night. Sure, she'd been given a bed and every comfort, but she was locked inside. By his order.

She banged her hand impotently against the wall, threw herself into the chair, and put her head in her hands. She knew what he was doing, because wouldn't she have done the same in his shoes? She was his enemy. It was that simple; it was that complicated.

Suddenly the door opened, and she jumped up. The two security guards who stood outside her room stepped to one side and saluted as a tall, white-robed man paused on the threshold before entering. The light behind him obscured his identity. All she was immediately aware of was his commanding presence, which emanated a simmering, barely controlled anger. She didn't need to see his face to identify him.

He'd come at last. It was the first time she'd seen him since her arrest. She'd wondered when he would. Roshan entered the room and closed the door. Previously, his admiring gaze had always moved around her body before settling on her eyes. Now, it went straight to her eyes like a laser beam intent on destruction. His anger was as cold and as heavy as iron. She'd have to be strong to withstand it.

She stood taller and swallowed. She felt nervous; she never felt nervous. But then she'd rarely been so wrong before. In his eyes, at least.

His dark eyes were as black and impenetrable as obsidian. They bored into her as if searching for a vulnerable soft spot which he could exploit, which he could understand, or which he could destroy. She didn't know which of these he wanted.

She opened her mouth to speak. She had intended to try to explain herself honestly. The day and night she'd been detained had forced her to search her soul and heart for the words that would convey the truth of what had happened and why. But looking at the man before her, she knew that he would not accept her explanation. And, instead of wanting to explain, she now felt a burst of anger in defense.

"How dare you keep me here!"

His lips curled into a sneer. "Now that isn't what I'd imagined you'd say."

She raised an eyebrow, her hands on her hips. "Ah, I guess you had me down for a sobbing mess, begging for your forgiveness. Well, you can forget that!"

"I was under no illusion you'd ask for forgiveness. The little I knew of you before I discovered your true identity proclaimed that. And then after, well, spies rarely beg for forgiveness. No, what I imagined you to do was use your sexuality to get around me, just as you did before."

She blenched at the thought that he truly believed that. But how could he believe otherwise? She shook her head.

"Good, at least I won't have to repel your unwanted advances."

She stepped away, unable to stop herself. He followed her, and she could step back no further when the edge of a table was in her way. She gripped on to it. He stood over her, his breathing coming faster, and his eyes warmer now. And, at that moment, she knew that he was lying. She wasn't repellent to him; he wanted her right now, just as he'd wanted her in their short time together. But no way was she about to weaken and allow her senses to take over. All that would do would be to prove to him that he was correct.

She forced herself to shrug. "What do you want, Roshan?" She deliberately spoke his name. She needed to get through to this stranger.

It seemed she did—temporarily. For a split second, the steeliness in his eyes vanished, and she saw something far worse—she saw someone hurting. She gave an involuntary gasp as the steeliness slammed firmly back into place once more.

"What I want, Shakira"—he practically spat out her name—"is the truth. Other than the fact that you are my enemy, and that you are a spy. Those things I know already."

She folded her arms in front of her. "You want to

know why I did it? Why I came to Sharq Havilah, why I had sex with you?" She wanted nothing more than to tell him the exact truth about what happened. Maybe then she'd shift the hateful barrier which he'd erected between them.

"No." The word exploded from his mouth like a gun. "I have no interest in why you slept with me for information, why you spied on me. The whys and wherefores are of no importance. There's only one thing I want to know, and that is to whom you've passed the information that you found on my computer."

She opened her mouth to speak, but it was suddenly dry. "I have told no one."

He laughed, a short, sharp laugh of total derision. "And you expect me to believe that?"

She lifted her chin. "Yes, I do."

He shook his head and paced away, then turned and glared at her. "You gatecrash my palace, you seduce me, you take photos of my private quarters, and take information from my computer and you *don't* tell anyone? Come on, Shakira. You don't expect me to believe that."

"I do. Because it's the truth."

He paced back to stand in front of her again, his eyes hot with anger. "I don't believe you'd know the truth if you walked into it, if it stood in front of you, threatening you."

"Like you are, you mean?"

Of all the things she could have said, that appeared to have got to him. Suddenly the anger that had only briefly vanished when she'd said his name dissolved from his eyes, and he half-turned away, raking his fingers through his hair.

"I do not threaten you." His voice was broken and low. He twisted back to face her. The anger had gone from his eyes, leaving something she had never seen there before, something she would have described as vulnerability, in any other circumstances.

"Then what do you do?"

"I repeat, I want to know the truth."

A bitter laugh escaped her lips. "Then we had better be seated because it will take a long time to tell you."

"We have all the time in the world." From the weary tone of his voice, it sounded as if that time seemed like an eternity to him.

She bit her lip to stop it from trembling, as his vulnerability threatened her strength. He might be hurt by her actions, but he held all the cards now. He could change at the drop of a hat, and she could be imprisoned for the rest of her life. She had to be strong.

"May I sit down?"

His face was grim as he waved his hand, indicating she could be seated.

She walked slowly to the sofas, ignoring the more formal office table and chairs. She needed Roshan relaxed so she could reach him. It was her only chance. Because all the evidence pointed to her spying, and she needed him to believe in her and what she was saying if she was ever to be released from captivity.

She smoothed down her dress and crossed her ankles. Roshan took the seat opposite her, the glass coffee table between them acting as a barrier. He sat on the edge of his seat, his hands clasped loosely before him, his eyes fixed on her with concentration.

"Begin."

The command did not bode well for a two-way conversation. She drew in a long breath as she tried to figure out where to begin. She decided to start with the worst of it.

"We were born to hate each other, Roshan," she said, in a soft undertone.

He grunted for her to continue. Whether he agreed with her statement or not, she could not tell. But he could not doubt its veracity.

She looked down at her hands, which were interlaced, her thumbs rubbing together, as she tried to think through the morass of crimes that each country, each family, had committed to the other.

"I was fourteen when your family murdered my mother and brothers." She glanced up at him, but he didn't seem to have registered her words. "The snipers picked them off with ease." She swallowed and closed her eyes as the memory of that day threatened to swamp her. "They would have shot me, too, if I hadn't been such a tomboy. I was in the sea. The others were on the beach, easily identifiable as the royal family." She grunted an unamused laugh. "I must have seemed just like a random passerby as I ran up to the beach to see what was going on. So, I was spared." She opened her eyes. "Spared from death, but not from grief. I vowed there and then that I would do anything to avenge their deaths."

She'd told the worst of it. She paused as she tried to gather her grief and tumult of feelings together, to carry on. Because he was right—now was the time for truth, and this was only the beginning of it. But then he did something surprising.

He brought his hands together in a slow clap. "What a

performance." He sat back on the chair, his eyes narrowing with derision. "I had not thought you would resort to that."

"This is no performance. This is my reality, a reality I've had to live with every day of these past ten years."

"And this sorry story is the reason why you slept with me—to avenge family. You price yourself too low, my dear."

"You're wrong," she said quietly. "Believe it or not, I had no idea of your identity. All I knew was that we had made a connection. All I knew was that I was sick of who I was and what I'd been instructed to do. All I knew was that I wanted to do something for myself for a change. I wanted to be young and have fun, and so… I indulged myself. Which is something I have rarely done in my life before, believe it or not."

There must have been something in her words that had reached him. She didn't have the first idea of what it was. But it was there in his eyes. The look of uncertainty flickered over his face, and his eyes scrunched a little.

"I do believe that. You didn't know who I was. And we did have a connection." He shook his head. "But the reason you were there was to spy on me."

"I had no choice. My brother insisted. I agreed, knowing I would only go through the motions, so I could return to the country I love. I am sick of this life. I am sick of the constant warring between our countries. I'm sick of the hatred. I want it all to go away. What I wanted was pleasure." She looked up, and his eyes, which had grown more sympathetic. "And I got it."

He briefly leaned in toward her and then sat back again, as if correcting himself. He gave a gruff laugh and then rose and strode over to the window, which looked out across the garden where they'd first made love.

"As did I." But his eyes didn't linger on the garden. Instead, he looked up, across the rooftops to the distant city and the blue line of the sea. "But pleasure is never enough for people in our position." He turned to face her. "Because, despite your 'common' name, Shakira, I know you to be the daughter of the royal family of Jazira. Another thing you are correct about. We were born to be enemies." He pressed his lips together briefly and nodded. "Your countrymen killed my parents."

"I used to think that, but now I believe it wasn't my countrymen. It was mercenaries hired by my brother."

"They were under Jaziran control," he said coldly. "And then the death of your mother and brothers. We were held responsible and, in our anger, we didn't deny it. But we weren't responsible. Our spies tell us that it was your brother, Nabeel, and his conspirators."

Shakira gasped. "You're wrong."

"No. Nabeel wanted the way clear to rule after your father's death. You, too, we understand, were on the list. As you say, you weren't with the others and so you were spared."

"And I've been living on borrowed time ever since." She shook her head. "I can't believe it, any of it."

He shrugged. "That's up to you. But it's the truth, albeit a complicated one. Our lives have been built on hatred, and that hatred was created for a purpose—greed and power."

Her world seemed to tilt on its axis as she absorbed the full meaning of Roshan's words. She'd been hating the wrong people all her life. Shakily, she thrust her fingers through her hair, and looked up at him.

"So much hatred. Do you want to know the real reason I had sex with you in the garden? Because I wanted to feel something other than that hatred."

She was shocked when he reached out and gently touched her cheek. "Then we are even more like each other than I imagined."

"Can we not stop the hatred here, now, Roshan? With us? We are like each other. We're both as bad and as good as each other. We could begin a change between our countries."

He took her hand, and for a moment, he looked at it as if torn whether to kiss it or let it drop. He let it drop. "My advisors anticipated you would attempt to reconcile. I didn't believe them. I didn't believe you to be so naive that you would ignore our charges against you and play on the personal." He shook his head. "It won't work. We need to know exactly what you've done."

"I've done nothing I'm ashamed of."

"I didn't imagine for a minute that you had. What I want to know is what you've done. Whether you're ashamed of it, or not, is of no interest, or consequence, to me."

She sat down. "Okay, I'll start from the beginning."

"If you must." He sat opposite her again.

"After my mother and brothers died, I spent my time with my father and brother, and their hatred of your country and your family infected me. But at nineteen my grandmother insisted I should study in England. I didn't want to go, and I didn't see why I should go. Neither did my father or brother, but my grandmother was held in high esteem by my father, and I was allowed to leave, providing I returned immediately after I graduated."

"Your grandmother was one of the more rational members of your family."

She shot him a black look, then realized he was correct and sighed. "She died last year, shortly before my father died of a heart attack. My brother recalled me to Jazira before my studies were complete. My brother insisted I return to Jazira and accept the marriage he has arranged. But that, en route, I should glean some information from you."

Roshan sat back. "You were charged with taking photographs of my private quarters. You were charged with breaking into my laptop and stealing whatever documents you could about our military and defenses."

She bit her lip and nodded. A heavy silence filled the air.

"And did you?" he asked.

"No. Although I know it looks like it. I didn't know your identity when we went into the garden. You must know that."

He gave a curt nod of the head.

"And when I took that photo, it was a selfie to remember the night by. That was all."

The muscles twitched in his jaw. "Either that, or you were an extremely inept spy."

She huffed a brief laugh. "Both, I think. Whatever you believe, I wasn't born to hate. I wasn't born to spy. Those moments with you were ones that I thought would be my last of freedom and fun. They were moments for me—not for my family or country. You must believe me."

Again the brief, stern nod to the head. "But that doesn't explain why you were looking at my phone."

"It was innocent initially. An incoming message which I automatically looked at. And then I saw my photo and I wanted to delete it. I couldn't risk it falling into my brother's hands.

"Why not? I thought that was the purpose of your visit—to seduce me and get me close enough to find out state secrets?"

"It was. But if my brother had ever seen those images, he'd have known that I'd failed in my mission."

His frown deepened. "How so?"

She shrugged. "There was no disguising how happy I was."

She reached over and took his hand. She had to get through to him. "Roshan, you must believe me, I was drawn to you the instant I met you—that had nothing to do with why I was sent here, and everything to do with what we were to each other. Everything."

He narrowed his eyes and withdrew his hand. "You think that if you touch me, my attitude will soften towards you?"

Her heart fell. She couldn't bear to see him so cold towards her. She shrugged. "Maybe. Although I don't think your heart is as hard as you suggest. You could have had me thrown into your roughest jail. You could have had me interrogated by professional guards. You could have done anything to me, and yet you have not. You've kept me safe."

He smiled then, but it was a smile that chilled her.

"And you think this to be kindness on my part?" He shook his head. "No, it's pity. I could do anything to you, as you say, but there's little point. You'll receive that kind of treatment when you return home. I'm doing you a favor, Shakira, by keeping you here."

The chill sank deeper into her soul. She licked her dry lips. "What are you talking about?"

"Simply that, if you return home, you will not be trusted by anyone. You'll be perceived to be a double agent, working for me. Or are you? There will always be doubt, always distrust on both sides about you. They'll say: *but weren't you kept in the luxury of the palace? Didn't your lover interrogate you? And how, Shakira, they will ask, exactly were you imprisoned? Exactly what punishment or torture did you endure?* You claimed to be homeless before, but now, my dear, you truly are."

They locked eyes for a few long moments when she felt the return of his hostility. She wasn't surprised because she knew him well enough to know that he had no alternative but to suppress his feelings if he was going to deal with her as a traitor to his country should be dealt with.

Roshan looked away first, as if he couldn't bear to see her any longer. He rose with one swift movement and opened the door where two guards stood, either side of the door.

She was about to follow him, as she usually would—after all, she'd never been imprisoned in her life before—when he turned and gestured to her to stay where she was. She stopped abruptly in the middle of the room.

"You're leaving," she said in a dull tone. "Without me."

"It's customary," he said, with a steeliness in his voice, "for the jailor to leave the jail, and the prisoner within it to remain confined."

"I thought you wanted the truth. I've given you the truth. What else do you hope to get from me that you haven't already got?"

"You're right. I did want the truth. But now I want something more. I want information."

"Information, about what?"

"Anything and everything that will weaken Jazira and strengthen Sharq Havilah."

"I will not give you anything else," she said in a low voice. "Jazira is my country, my family, and my countrymen and women. I will not betray them."

"You already have," he said, quietly closing the door behind him.

As he walked away, he clenched and unclenched his hands. His body was riven with tension—tension between the anger he felt at her disloyalty and the deep-rooted passion he felt for her, which still raged inside him. He didn't want to feel those bone-deep emotions; he didn't want to have any feelings whatsoever. He'd believed them to be extinguished. He'd believed that the place where his heart should have been was a void created by the violence between Jazira and his country.

It had made him harder on her than he should have been. Because it wasn't her he was angry with, but himself. And that anger made him all the more determined to gain as much information from her as he could to conquer her country once and for all. And it also made him all the more determined to ensure he didn't allow his feelings to surface ever again.

~

SHAKIRA PACED THE FLOOR. She had seen no one in two days, no doubt to emphasize her position. But if he thought it would soften her up into telling him everything about her country, he had another think coming.

All the isolation had done was to make her realize that she would never again be a pawn in men's games.

So when the knock came, she was surprised. It was early evening, and she had been expecting her dinner to be delivered. Instead, it was Roshan, the dark shadows under his eyes telling her all she needed to know of his suffering and sleepless nights. She jumped up, immediately wanting to hold him, to see if he was all right. She stopped herself just in time.

"Your story checks out," he said briefly.

"It was no story." She held his gaze steadily. "It was the truth. I've never lied to you."

"Only by omission," he said, his tired, hot eyes, searching hers. "Which is worse. Lies that are out in the open are more easily detected. Lies that are hidden, unsaid, are treacherous. It makes you untrustworthy."

She pursed her lips as her heart broke.

"Some of my ministers want me to continue to keep you incarcerated," he continued.

"And others?"

"Suggest an alternative. An alternative I'm inclined to agree with."

Her heart beat rapidly. Please, God, give her freedom. "And what is that alternative?"

"For you to stay in Sharq Havilah as my guest. We

cannot risk you returning to your own country. You know too much, and your own life would be at risk."

"Here, in the palace?"

"Yes, it is the only place you are truly safe."

Her heart leaped again. He did want to continue their relationship. "And we will be together."

He shook his head. "There will be no repetition of my earlier foolishness. I will marry Sheikha Elaheh of Tawazun, and there will be no kind of relationship between us."

"Then why keep me here?"

He grimaced and turned away. "It's for your own safety. What you've done, playing me off against your brother—"

"I did nothing of the sort—"

"What you've done," he repeated firmly, refusing to allow her to speak, "has jeopardized not only my country's security but your own. Until we can be assured of your safety, you may stay here as my guest. After some time has passed, if your brother indicates you will be safe, you may return to England to continue your studies." He waved his hand dismissively. "Or whatever else you wish to do."

She nodded. "Okay." There was a long pause, and she willed him to look at her. "Roshan, I'm sorry. I'm so sorry for everything. I didn't mean it to be like this."

"No, I dare say you didn't. Neither of us did."

She reached across and took his hand. "Can we think of a way forward? Where we can put the hatred behind us? Find a new path for our countries?"

His grim expression answered her question. He sighed and shook his head, and when he did look at her, she wished he hadn't. She almost recoiled under his cold but troubled gaze.

"I don't know, Shakira. This is a mess. I thought the tension between our countries was bad. It's worse than ever now. Something major has to happen to make things right. All I can do is provide you with a safe place to stay until all of this dies down, and you are safe from your brother."

She nodded. Her brother was notoriously ruthless. She knew that he would both be suspicious and furious with her over what had happened. He had also become increasingly unpredictable and erratic since her father's death. She knew Roshan was right.

They stood silently looking at each other for a few seconds. The air was heavy with emotion and tension. She gasped when he finally walked to the door and exited without looking back.

She sat slowly on the chair and held her head in her hands. What had she done? What had her yearning for a normal life cost her and both of their countries?

THE WEEKS HAD PASSED, each hour of every day moving unmarked into the next. She rarely saw Roshan. Her only link to the outside world was a regular daily update from Roshan's office on relations between the two countries, what she read online, and the small amounts of gossip she could glean from the women who attended her. It all amounted to very little. On the face of it, it seemed that her brother had little interest in her, and nor did the world. Which was exactly how she liked it.

What she didn't like was that Roshan also appeared to have little interest in her. He'd made no visits, no phone calls, no communication whatsoever. What he'd said to her as he'd left her haunted her mind. He couldn't trust her, and his life would go on without her. And it seemed he'd meant what he'd said.

So where did that leave her? She paused by the window through which the sea breeze entered and looked longingly across the city to the sea. She closed her eyes and imagined the caress of the warm water over her skin, like a lover. She was a physical person, and she longed for sensation.

She opened her eyes. Where did that leave her? Alone. She was the only person who would look out for her, who knew her, the only person who knew what she needed. And she needed to break out of this captivity—now.

A few hours later, she'd managed to evade the guards who had become more lax since the change in her status from prisoner to someone to be protected. No one, it seemed, would imagine that she would risk her own life. But, as she slipped through the outer compound, disguised in the abaya and hijab of a servant, she soon found herself outside in the busy capital, amongst the people she'd missed.

As she inhaled the sights, sounds, and smells of the city, she began to feel calmer. She entered the market, drawn by the bustling activity after so long on her own. She had no money to buy anything but, after conversing with the stallholders, she found herself grinning as she emerged from the market with a handful of dates. She continued to the dock area where she sat on the end of a pier, munched on the dates, and contemplated the hazy island way out to sea—her homeland.

Roshan was concerned for her safety, imagining her brother wanted her home. But she knew her brother. As a young prince, he'd been an ordinary boy, shyer than her, for sure, and uncertain of himself. She'd looked out for him. Despite how he'd changed in recent years, she couldn't imagine he would hurt her.

No, she thought, he'd be too busy fighting with his army and his counselors with whom, it seemed, he rarely agreed.

She was grateful that in Roshan's country, the laws were freer over women and dress. Women walked around in western clothes, with scarves casually wrapped around their heads, while others preferred to wear a full burka. Neither were restrained from doing what they liked in this liberal country. A far cry from her own, she thought, as she leaned back on her hands, face upturned to the sun. She pushed down the hijab to allow the sun to caress her face. She couldn't help smiling up at it, relishing its heat and light against her skin. It did nothing to relieve the numbness in her heart but made her feel a little more alive.

Suddenly a bright light shone in her eyes, and she turned in a panic in the direction from where the light had come. But she could see nothing. She sat upright and scanned the quay but couldn't see anything around the group of huts from which she could have sworn the light came.

Then she realized that the quayside was quieter than usual. The hours had passed, and it was now the time when workers departed for prayers, rest, and food. She rose but couldn't get rid of a strange feeling down her spine, which prickled as if she was being watched.

Ridiculous, she said to herself as she began to retrace her steps, except this time she decided to return to the palace by the most direct route. What had started as a compelling need to enjoy a sense of freedom, hear the sea slapping against the sea wall, smell the salty air and hear the conversations of people who weren't palace courtiers, had ended with a barely suppressed feeling of panic. That feeling sent adrenalin into her limbs as her walk quickened. There was no way around it. She had to pass the sheds from where that spark of light had come—a spark of light, much like binoculars trained on her.

She saw something move quickly out of the corner of her eye, and gasped and began to run. She hadn't even reached the end of the huts when she heard the pounding of footsteps—many footsteps—and two men grabbed her arms.

She screamed, but it was cut short as a cloth was clamped over her mouth, and she struggled as a chemical smell overtook her. The last thing she remembered was the power draining from her limbs and the world turning upside down as she was tossed over the shoulder of one of the men. Her last sight was the receding city and the roar of a motorboat as they sped across the sea, away from Sharq Havilah and Roshan, out toward the island of Jazira.

"WHERE IS SHE?" demanded Roshan, pacing the floor as he tried to deny the dread which had sunk into his bones when he'd first been informed that Shakira was missing.

There were shrugs from everyone except his premier advisor, Hasan, who cleared his throat.

"We don't know for sure, Your Highness, but we've received reports that she went to the market before lunch, and she was seen sitting at the end of the quay. No one remembers her returning. But they do remember a motorboat and a group of strangers taking off suddenly at around that time."

"She's been taken by Jazira."

It was as if all the blood had drained from him. But it didn't weaken him, it seemed to make him stronger. What he needed to do flashed into his mind, and he fired off lists of instructions to his team. They were soon running around, setting his plan into action.

Because, whatever Shakira had done, or not done, of one thing he was sure—she was in mortal danger in Jazira with her brother. And he had no option but to get her out.

He could no more turn his back on her than on himself. Like it or not, she was a part of him now.

CHAPTER 7

For two days, Shakira was kept hidden in the depths of the Jazira palace. The ancient castle was riddled with secret passageways, the result of thousands of years of intrigue and smuggling and secrecy. But, while the chambers she inhabited were old, they were also luxurious—filled with silks and velvets and precious textiles stolen over the centuries from passing ships. The prison might be luxurious, but she was still a prisoner, unable to leave her quarters, unable to receive visitors.

She paced the large room, of which she'd been the sole occupant since she'd arrived. No one had been allowed near her. She'd never felt so alone in her own country. All she knew was that her brother was keeping her waiting, trying to break her before he saw her because he knew she hated feeling trapped. What she didn't know was what he planned to do with her.

She paused by the window and looked out again, focusing on the ancient weather-beaten walls crumbling under the mass of greenery. She watched as a bird flew out from a nest up into the sky. She followed it upwards until it became a dot, and her eyes watered. Then she tore her eyes away. She shouldn't taunt herself with freedom. Not yet. But she was determined to get it. As soon as her brother, Nabeel, offered one small chink in the security that encased her, she would take advantage of it and get out of here. She just had to be on her guard.

Suddenly there was rapping on the door.

"Enter."

The guards opened the door and bowed to her. Despite Nabeel's cruel ways, or even because of them, it seemed his guards held her in high respect. They never entered her room unless she bade them enter, and they always acted with the utmost deference. It was no different now.

"Our Princess. His Highness requests that you come immediately to the discussion chamber."

"Requests?" She arched her eyebrow. "Somehow, I doubt he requested."

The guards merely lowered their eyes. They did not dare agree with her as that would show disloyalty to her brother, the king. But their expressions revealed that she was correct. Not for the first time, she wondered at their apparent loyalty to her. Maybe her brother's stranglehold on their country wasn't so invincible after all.

She smoothed down her abaya and adjusted her hijab in the mirror. Heavily kohled eyes looked back at her. She'd decided immediately she'd returned to Jazira that her best hope was to return to the traditional. Gone were the scanty clothes, the western hair, and makeup. In their place stood a serious woman who represented her country. "But I will come nevertheless." She turned and smiled at the two guards who were looking at her with kindly eyes.

"I am sorry, Princess, that you are being treated this way. If—"

She raised a hand to stop him from speaking. She didn't want him to incriminate himself. "You need say nothing further. I understand. And I will never forget your loyalty." She glanced at the open door and wondered if she was about to step out into freedom, or into something opposite—something that might be far worse.

Shakira walked through the door where more guards were waiting. They too saluted and stepped respectfully to one side. Something had happened, she sensed it. Maybe her brother had gone too far this time in capturing one of his own.

She couldn't help noting the differences to Roshan's palace as she walked along the corridor. Here the walls seemed to whisper with the past. The marks and imprints of ancient, and not so ancient, clashes—scars in the stone, scorch marks from fires—and the passing through of centuries of generations of her people, were scored in the walls and the dipped stone of the passageway.

The ruins of war were also visible in the gardens where cannonballs had shattered fountains that had been poorly mended and whose scars were still visible. But above the ravaged stone were the huge trees, planted centuries before, which jutted into the sky as if determined to assert hope for the future. Shakira clung to that hope. She needed every shred she could find to face her brother.

Eventually, they arrived at the part of the palace where the royal family resided. It was newer and had been better maintained than the rest, as if the family was only concerned with itself—not its people or anything which didn't affect it directly. Shakira had never reflected on this before, but now she did. It hurt her to the core that her family had been so insular, so uncaring of anything other than itself.

But she had no time to consider this further before she was ushered into a small meeting room which she'd never before entered. The guards stood all around her, looking out rather than at her. It wasn't clear whether they were there to secure her or to defend her. She got the feeling it was the latter, for which she was grateful. They waited silently, facing double doors through which, she knew instinctively, her brother would make an entrance.

Without warning, the doors burst open, and her brother, Nabeel, entered the room. He was of a similar height to her, shorter than the men around him. But his hard eyes glittered as they looked upon her. He'd been weak as a young boy, but that weakness had now transmuted into meanness. And, it seemed, her guards had known this before she had and were there to protect her as much as guard her. Things had changed a lot in a year.

"So here she is, my naughty little sister," he said, with a sneer. He beckoned his personal guards closer. She'd heard he never went anywhere without this small but powerful coterie of thugs, but hadn't believed it until now. Things had changed so much since her parents' day. Her father had been hard, but he had been intelligent enough to know he had to listen to his people and advisors, even if he didn't agree with them, and sometimes act on unwelcome advice. Her father had judgment; her brother had none. And it was just the two of them now.

She didn't consider his comments needed a response. She gazed at him with a firm expression until he looked away. He'd always been the first to look away. The reminder gave her strength. Her only hope was to maintain the authority she used to have when they'd been children together.

"How dare you have your men capture me, drug me, and bring me here against my wishes!"

"I dare because I am king and you betrayed me!" There was no hint of the meek boy he'd once been, but she refused to give in.

"And I am a Jaziran princess, and I demand your respect as my brother and king!"

"Respect? You disobeyed my orders. You didn't get the information we wanted, and, instead, no doubt gave Roshan plenty in return."

"I did nothing of the kind!" They stared at each other in a stand-off, and she saw, for a moment, a glimpse of the boy she'd known growing up. She drew in a deep breath. "This has got to stop, Nabeel. You cannot continue to run roughshod over your people, nor your family. You are terrorizing everybody."

His hand banged furiously against the table, sending shuddering shockwaves along it to her. She gripped its edges firmly to hide her flutter of fear. She didn't believe she was dealing with a sane man anymore.

"How dare you say such things! "

"I dare because they are the truth. You sent me to Sharq Havilah to find secrets that would help you undermine its king and his country. All I found was the truth. You have used pirates to pillage, steal, and harass the Havilahi countries."

Again came the slap of his hand upon the desk. It didn't scare her this time. "I've merely been doing what my father has done for years. Retribution for what they did to us!"

"He didn't do it like this. He didn't kill people for no reason. He didn't oppress our people as you are doing." She felt the guards behind her shuffle as if readying themselves the something—what, she didn't know.

"Shakira!" he snapped. "Carry on like this, and you will be returned to prison indefinitely."

"You need to hear the truth. Unless I tell you, no one else will. You have to stop this reign of terror. You are turning your people against you. And all eyes of our neighboring countries are upon you. You have become the most hated person in the region."

"What do I care about that? It is time they feared a Jaziri king. My father was too weak. I will not be. I will not make the same mistake."

"They might not be the same mistakes, but believe me, Nabeel, they are far greater mistakes than any our father made. You have to stop this. Now!"

"I did not bring you here to scold me as our mother did. I brought you here to discover what secrets you told that lover of yours in Havilah. I need to know what you have divulged, and you will tell me."

"How could I have told Roshan anything of importance? I know nothing. You, and my father before you, kept me misinformed. I believed our father when he told me how evil our neighbors were, and I believed you. I was a fool."

"And you are a bigger fool now. You are one of us, and

you will tell me what I need to know, even if I have to force you."

Her knuckles whitened as she gripped the side of the table and leaned forward to stare at him. "You would not dare touch me."

He looked her coolly up and down. "Despite your… obvious attractions, dear sister, I would not sully my hands with touching you."

Bile rose in her throat and threatened to make her choke. "You disgust me."

She felt the men around her tense. Nabeel rose and leaned forward, echoing her stance, gripping the table across from her. "And you, sister, are no longer a princess, honored and feted. You are a nobody who will continue to be imprisoned until you tell me all you know." He sat down again and chewed his nail, his agitation betrayed by facial twitches.

She drew in a deep breath, determined to ignore his insults. What was worse was that she was in danger of being told to leave without getting what she wanted. She had to get through to him.

"Nabeel," she said, her voice gentled as if trying to calm a flighty horse. She tried to appeal to the boy he once was, not the fleshy man whose mad eyes betrayed his increasing mania. "Please, listen to me. I am your sister. I am a Jaziran princess. Believe me when I say I gave Roshan no information. I would not betray my country like that."

He poked his angry face toward her. "I do not believe you. You betrayed me, and you betrayed my country."

She shook her head. "I did nothing of the sort. I went to Sharq Havilah as you bid me, but what I found there was like nothing I expected. Nabeel, they are our enemy no longer. You are living in the past. We need to make a change."

For a moment, it could have swung either way, and she held her breath, watching his every movement to decipher which way the ax would fall. Then he did something she hadn't expected; he laughed, and walked around her, inspecting her as if she were some unknown thing. Her heart sank.

He clapped his hands slowly. "My sister, always taking the high road. You always did believe you are better than us—the rest of your family—than me, your king!" His lip curled into a snarl, and she had to repress a shudder. Any sign of weakness would be pounced upon. Her only hope was to remind him of their family connections and to demand respect.

"You're wrong, Nabeel. I've never believed I'm better than anyone else in my family."

"Don't give me that," he spat out, before reaching in his jacket for a cigarette and lighting it. He took a drag, eyes narrowed as they surveyed her, and plucked a piece of tobacco from his tongue with a shaking hand. His drinking was getting worse, thought Shakira. "You've always looked down on our family since you were old enough to understand how we'd acquired our wealth."

She shook her head. "I didn't look down on them. But you're right, I did, and do, reject how they acquired their wealth. And how you still do. Piracy was something my grandfather and his forebears did in centuries gone by when times were lawless. They are no longer like that. You have to stop this."

"I'm not changing anything." He gesticulated wildly,

his hands flailing as if he couldn't control them. Shakira swallowed. He pointed in the direction of Sharq Havilah. "Those people with whom you've been consorting are our enemies, Shakira! You slept with our enemy! Have you forgotten it was they who were responsible for the deaths of our mother and brothers? Have you?"

"I haven't forgotten. But things are never as black and white as they seem."

He shook his head in disbelief. "You believe his lies?"

"I… believe what he told me, yes. These people are no longer our enemies, Nabeel. It's time to change. You could do it."

"No longer our enemies," he said slowly, shaking his head. "I was right, and my ministers were wrong. You are a double spy. Purporting to work for us when, in fact, you've told our enemy all our secrets."

"I told them nothing. I don't even know anything!" She took a deep breath. She had to get through to him. "Listen to me, Nabeel. We could work together to bring change to our country. If you don't want me involved, then fine, do it by yourself. Either way, it's time to change. Time to forget the past and create a stronger future, one that isn't based on hatred."

He frowned as if unsure for a few moments before taking another drag of his cigarette. "My people wouldn't stand for it."

"Your people would respect you for it."

"And what do you know of my people and what they want?"

He came closer, and she could smell the alcohol on his breath, his dilated pupils suggesting he'd mixed it with drugs. He shouldn't be in charge of himself, let alone a country. The thought gave her strength.

"Enough. I know enough to see our people want a change. I hear things."

He grunted dismissively, but the edgy look in his eyes showed that she'd caught his attention.

"I know there are people within and outside the palace who want change," she continued. "All you have to do is make that change, and the people will be behind you."

"Why should I, hey? It worked for my ancestors, it'll work for me."

She shook her head. "No longer, Nabeel. We live in different times, and we can live differently now."

Suddenly he softened, and he took a lock of her hair and pushed it away. At that moment, she saw her brother, weak and helpless, always looking to her for guidance.

"We can do it, you and me, together," she urged. For a long moment, everything hung in the balance as their gaze held, and shared memories swamped them. Then she made a mistake. She smiled. And his eyes instantly darkened.

He pushed her away. "You're laughing at me. Just like you and Mama always used to."

She shook her head. "No, we didn't."

"Yes, you all did. Mama wanted her son to be big and strong, like Papa. I tried, Shakira, but I'm not like him. But I found a way to be strong."

"Through force," she said dully, knowing she'd lost him.

He smiled then. "Exactly. And I intend to continue as I began. There will be no change in my country while I am king, and until you can understand that, you stay here—

locked up. You're too much a threat and danger to me to be allowed to escape."

Even if she'd believed she could get through to him—which she didn't, it was too late now, the moment had passed—she knew that any pleading would have the opposite effect on him. So she stood tall as he hesitated by the entrance. He turned to her.

"You could have always declined my command to go to Sharq Havilah."

She huffed a sarcastic laugh. "And what would you have done if I had?"

His lips curled into a cruel, self-satisfied smile. "You'd never have seen Jazira again."

"Exactly. You gave me no choice. My heart is, and always has been, in Jazira."

His smile broadened. "At least you understand that much. You have no choice but to do as I command."

She stepped toward him, her guards moving with her. "I may have agreed to go, but it was never my intention to spy for you or my country. I was never going to do that."

His expression hardened once more, and he shook his head. "You can't stop making things harder for yourself, can you?" He glanced at her guards. "Take her away and make sure you get the information I want from her."

Shakira couldn't wait to get away because she feared her brother more than the men who surrounded her. But as she walked out into the quiet twilight evening, which was suddenly getting dark, like a curtain drawn across the day, their pace quickened. Shakira suddenly felt alarmed. They weren't returning to her quarters, but to an even older part of the palace, where she knew prisoners had once been kept. It was unsavory, it was crumbling, and it had always been a place to be feared.

As they opened a door, she stopped and refused to enter. She turned to the head guard. "Where are you taking me?"

He glanced around, and there were her brother's personal bodyguards not far away. "You are to be interrogated. So we are taking you to the inner interrogation chamber."

A wave of nausea filled her, as she remembered the tales which had been told to her by her cousins to frighten her, of the goings-on in the prison over the centuries. She used to wake up, screaming from the nightmares.

She took one last glance at the gardens and took a deep breath of the fragrant air, wondering when she would breathe its sweet smell again. Then she turned to the guard and nodded. He stepped to one side, and she walked down into the dank corridor, the door clanging closed behind her.

They walked on and on through places she had never been but had heard enough about to never want to visit. Just when she was beginning to think they would never reach the horrors of the jail, her guards turned and entered a different corridor, and she felt the stone floor beginning to curve upwards. She didn't say anything but calculated that they must have reached beyond the palace grounds now, and if they were climbing, then they must be moving towards the mountainous interior of the island.

They approached more guards, and Shakira braced herself. The two sets of guards didn't exchange words. But as soon as they were in sight, the new guards acted swiftly and tossed a package to her chief guard. He extracted from it a black niqab—the kind market widows would wear, discreet, ordinary, unremarkable, which covered everything except their eyes.

"You want me to wear a niqab in jail?"

"No, Princess, we wish you to wear a niqab as you make your escape. You will be making it without us, we would attract too much attention. Your best disguise, it has been decided, is to be invisible in plain sight."

She gave a half-laugh, expressing both disbelief and relief. "Invisible in plain sight—the plight of so many of my countrywomen. And this escape has been designed by you?"

"I do not have that honor, Princess. A higher authority has arranged it. The less you know, the better. All you need to know is that you are safe. Listen carefully."

And Shakira did. As the precious minutes rolled by, she listened to the repeated instructions which told her exactly where to go, and for how long, and what to expect. After she'd escaped the confines of the palace grounds, she would be met and taken somewhere safe. Safe, she repeated to herself. She couldn't remember the last time she felt safe, apart from when she was with Roshan.

"Are you ready, Princess?"

She nodded. "I am. I will not forget you and your fellow guards' help."

"There are more of us who support you, Princess. Most of us. Things will change soon and quickly. And then we will call you. Your country needs you, not your brother, never your brother. We are loyal only to you now."

This was a change that she had not expected. But she had no time to consider his words. She left the confines of the building and was immediately swamped by thick darkness and overgrown trees. She did as she was told and followed the path upward, identifying the landmarks which had been described to her. She was outside the palace but still in danger. She could hear dogs barking from the palace grounds, and hoped that her guards were safe. She didn't know how they were going to keep the fact that she had escaped from her brother. But when it was known, she knew that all hell would break loose in their country.

She stumbled up the hill and, turning suddenly, ran straight into something solid, and then an arm reached out and grabbed her. She opened her mouth to scream, but a second hand clamped over her mouth, and she was pulled hard against a man's body, unable to move, unable to breathe, unable to see anything in the blackness which consumed her.

CHAPTER 8

"Quiet!" The command was issued low and urgent. A tingle of recognition ran down her spine, her body reacting before her brain. She twisted her head to try to see her captor, but he held her tight. "Quiet," he repeated, softer now, in a tone she recognized. "Will you be quiet?" She nodded under his hand, and he released her. She turned round to face her captor, her brain finally catching up with what all her senses were telling her.

"Roshan?" she whispered, pulling aside the niqab. "Is it truly you?"

He brushed his hand over her cheek in a swift caress to reassure her of his reality. He brought his mouth to her ear, his warm breath tickling her skin. "None other," he whispered, with his familiar wry charm. He brought her to him in a swift, reassuring embrace before cupping her face with his hands and looking her in the eyes. "We don't have much time. Do as I say. Okay?"

She nodded, and he took her hand, and they emerged

cautiously onto a ridge. He checked his watch and scanned the darkness of the small fishing village which lay below them. They had to wait only a few moments before a light flickered twice.

"Ready?"

She nodded. They ran down the rough track, away from the rocky plateau with its shelter of shrubby bushes, toward a fishing village which was situated on the other side of the peninsula to the city and port. But before they reached the village, Roshan led her to a barren hook of land from which a few lone boats were moored. They crouched for a few moments behind a tumbledown fishing shed while Roshan carefully surveyed the scene.

"Now!" he said, and they ran to an ancient jetty and picked their way carefully along the narrow gangplank and onto the small fishing vessel. Roshan unhooked the rope, tossed it on board, and pulled the plank away from the jetty.

A red tip of a cigarette was all that could be seen of the boat's captain, who started the engine in response to a wave from Roshan. Shakira winced as the hum of the engine filled the small fishing bay. At first, they moved slowly, the chug of the boat throbbing in the night air, the land slipping behind them at a snail's pace. The offshore breeze picked up as they slowly and imperceptibly moved through the velvet waters of the famed Jazira Bay—once a place of classical fables, but now a place of danger. The peninsula, which separated the fishing village from the city and port, loomed darkly into view.

Shakira gripped the railings tightly as they passed the harbor's outer point, marked by a small lighthouse. She held her breath as the light from the lighthouse skimmed the water in front of them. She looked back at the city, with the palace brightly lit on the top. It was a dominating presence, oppressing not only its neighbors but now, she realized, also its inhabitants.

Roshan touched her arm. "Come away. It's too dangerous. We will pass within the beam of light shortly, and there could be snipers."

"Snipers?" She shook her head and pushed her hair away from her face, unable to suppress the grief of what was happening from surfacing. She'd kept it hidden for too long. "What has my once proud country come to?"

He didn't answer because the answer was clear. "Come, Shakira."

She didn't need to ask again. It wouldn't serve her, or her countrymen, to be killed by a sniper.

They descended the steps to the cabin below where she'd expected to see Roshan's security men. The cabin was empty.

"You've come alone?"

"It was the only way."

"I'm surprised your advisors let you." The look in his eyes told her all she needed to know. "Ah, they didn't. They don't know you're here."

"They do now. I have reinforcements waiting for us inside our territory. But, no, I didn't tell them before. They would never have agreed. They would have told me it made no sense."

"And they'd be right, wouldn't they? It doesn't make any sense. Tell me, Roshan, why did you come? Why did you risk so much for me?"

His dark eyes were unreadable in the gloom of the cabin. He closed the blinds and flicked on a light. His fingers held onto the lamp and slowly withdrew. "I couldn't let you stay there. The thought of what might happen to you…" He trailed off.

His dark eyes filled with something she would have interpreted as grief or confusion if she hadn't known him better. It stirred her in a raw place that felt vulnerable after being hidden for so long.

"I… I'm surprised after what I did. I thought you'd hate me."

He glanced at her before returning his focus to his phone. It was as if he was avoiding looking at her. "I did hate you," he finally ground out. When he turned, she saw that the grief and confusion had vanished, and the reason he was hiding was that there was an entirely new expression in his eyes. And she certainly didn't know what to call that. "But I find I couldn't sustain it."

"You don't hate me anymore."

"No." He shrugged. "I find I can't."

She gave a weak laugh. "Well, I guess that's good."

His expression was serious now. "It certainly is good."

"How come?"

He shrugged. "I couldn't deny what I felt, and I felt the opposite of the things I said. I said I didn't trust you, and I do. I implied you meant nothing to me, but you do."

She swallowed, her heart too full for words. He twisted around awkwardly and raked his fingers through his hair. She'd never seen him make an inelegant movement before. She reached out and touched him. And he instantly stopped. They looked at each other silently for a few moments, and then he drew her to him and held her close. She rested her cheek against his chest and breathed deeply.

Suddenly there was an explosion, and they leaped apart.

"Stay here," he said, already opening the door. "Keep low, and don't come out unless you know it's me."

He slammed the door shut behind him and ran up the stairs. She switched off the lights and stared out the porthole, trying to see what had made the noise. She was at the rear of the boat, looking back toward the land. The motor had roared into top speed at the explosion, and water splashed up, partly obscuring her view. But then there was another flash of light and a bang above her. They were being fired at from the direction of the shore. She just hoped that they were firing from land and that their quickly accelerating boat would soon take them out of range.

She'd hoped in vain, she realized, as she looked up to see the intermittent bursts of light move closer. The gunmen were aboard a boat, and they were advancing on them, fast. It was all she needed to know. There were only three people aboard their boat, and one of them was driving it.

She flung open cupboards until she found what she needed—a gun. She'd been brought up hunting in the desert and had been taught how to use a gun at an early age. She ran up the stairs to emerge to a barrage of bullets thudding into the wood above her head. She tugged off her robes and, clad only in jeans and t-shirt, shimmied along the wet deck toward the rear of the boat where she could see Roshan kneeling in the bottom of the boat behind the raised stern. He rested his gun on the transom, pointing to where the gunmen were steadily approaching.

She landed with a thump beside him and, without a

word, slid her rifle alongside his. "You take the sniper to the left, I'll take the right one," she shouted, above the roar of the boat's engine.

She had to wedge herself steady as the boat bounced and buffeted on the water as they sped out of the shelter of the harbor, and into the rougher open seas.

"I told you to—" Whatever else Roshan was going to say was cut short by another blast of gunshot.

She ignored him, took aim, and fired her gun. There were no more explosions from the right side of the deck.

"Where did you learn to shoot like that?" shouted Roshan as he focused down the barrel of his gun and pulled the trigger. The Jaziran boat went black and fell silent. Roshan and Shakira continued to lie flat, the damp of the seawater seeping into her clothes and skin but the heat and adrenalin making her oblivious to its chill.

During those long moments when neither light nor sound penetrated the darkness of the strait, neither of them moved or looked at each other. Despite this, Shakira was utterly aware of Roshan. Her thigh was touching his. The heat of his body warmed her own. But he showed no acknowledgment of that—his concentration was absolute, as was hers.

There was another pop of fire from a different angle, and Roshan immediately fired at that point, but it continued. He ran out of ammunition and rolled onto his back and re-loaded his gun. He checked forward and saw the lights of Sharq Havillah and a flotilla of his own navy waiting for them.

"Another five minutes and we'll be safe."

She covered him while he re-loaded his gun. The boat seemed to be approaching faster now, as if aware that they had only minutes to retake their princess and return her to prison, doomed to a life of captivity.

Roshan shrank back and covered her with himself. "It's no good. We have to keep low. We're too close to fire now. They'd pick us off easily. Keeping out of sight is our only hope until we reach my waters."

She rested her cheek against the dirty and sodden bottom of the boat, pressed further by Roshan's weight, covering her, keeping her from harm at his expense. She wondered why he was doing this. His life was dearer than hers, a kingdom depended on it.

For long seconds, they bumped over the strait's choppy waves as the thrum of the Jaziran boat came ever closer. Just as she thought they would both perish under the fire of her countrymen, there was a roar of guns exploding from in front of them, and the boat behind erupted in flames. They'd entered Roshan's territory, and his navy had opened fire the second the Jaziran boat had entered their waters. The other, back-up Jaziran boats, no doubt manned by her brother's personal army, swerved suddenly and headed back to shore to tell their king that they'd failed to keep his sister in prison.

Only then did Roshan roll off Shakira. She lay soaked, her body shaking and unable to move, as the events of the night suddenly sunk in.

"Shakira?" Roshan asked, gently at first. But she couldn't reply, her teeth were chattering too much. "Shakira!" His voice was louder now. "Are you hurt?" She shook her head, but he couldn't see in the darkness. She was vaguely aware of the sounds of boats approaching, and of lights surrounding their boat.

Roshan gently put his hands under her and lifted her up, surveying her from top to toe, checking for wounds.

"Tell me, are you hurt?"

She shook her head but couldn't stop shivering.

"You're in shock, and soaked and chilled to the bone. Hold on, we'll soon have you to shore and safety."

Safety? She couldn't help wondering if she could ever be safe again when she was wanted in her own country—for all the wrong reasons—and not wanted in any other.

Someone handed Roshan a blanket, and he pulled it around her before stepping up to the jetty. She took one last look at the lights now far out to sea, and the distant darkness of her homeland, which she realized now she would always be a stranger to, before she was swept away into a waiting car to take them the short distance to the palace.

As soon as the car pulled up, she made herself sit up, and when the door opened, she jumped out and swept away Roshan's objections.

"I'll carry you," he said.

"No, I don't need carrying." She refused to be weak. But she didn't shrug off his arm when he slid it around her, holding her close and allowing her to lean against him.

Door after door was swept open before them, and they were soon in his suite of rooms. She refused to have a doctor check her over.

"I'm fine, really. I just need to shower and sleep." She twisted her hair back off her face and grimaced. "I'm just exhausted, Roshan. I just need to go to sleep."

After a brief pause, Roshan nodded and dismissed the waiting medics, closing the door behind them.

She stood gripping the side of the chair, partly to keep herself upright and partly to stop herself from returning to his arms where she felt so safe.

He frowned. "You look done in."

"You don't look so hot, either!"

He grinned, and the tension vanished. "You take the first shower while the food comes."

She didn't need telling twice. She went into the bathroom, flicked on the steaming shower, and peeled off her cold, wet clothes. As she stood under the stream of water, washing away the fear and dirt and chill of being forced to flee her own country, she couldn't stop the tears from rolling down her face. She leaned her forehead against the misty tiled wall, and her shoulders shook as she wrapped her arms around herself and tried to reconcile what had happened—she'd become an outcast of her own country.

ROSHAN FOUND her sobbing in the shower. Her beautiful, proud, naked body was bowed and supported by her hands and forehead, pressed against the cool tiles. It tore at his heart to see her like this and, without a second thought, he stepped fully clothed into the shower and flicked it off. He immediately pulled her into his arms to support her. She may have refused him once, but she was too vulnerable to resist a second time. He lifted her into his arms and carried her into the bedroom. He sat down and held her while she continued to sob. He smoothed her hair away from her face. He kissed her cheek, muttering soothing words into her ear until eventually she'd cried herself out. She sat up then and kissed him. He'd have liked nothing further than to make love to her, but now wasn't the time.

"Are you going to tell me what that was all about? Because it wasn't all shock, was it? I get the feeling something has been brewing within you for some time."

She shivered, and he pulled the duvet around her.

She nodded. "You're right. I think for the first time in my life, I've finally left my family behind. The shutters have fallen from my eyes, and I can truly see them for what they were, and what they have become. But it grieves me because my people are left under my brother's yoke, doing what he instructs them to do. And they don't like it. They're restless now. They, too, can see that their lives can and should be different." She sighed and rested her head against his forehead. "Oh, Roshan. What can I do?"

He breathed her in deeply until he felt as if she'd reached inside him as far as he could bring her, connecting with himself at the most elemental level. And for the first time in forever, he felt whole. Only then did he open his eyes, surprised at his feelings, and sure about his opinion.

Instead of answering, he lifted her aside and pulled back the sheet. "You should get into bed. You must be exhausted. All this can wait until tomorrow. We'll talk it through then."

She nodded and slid under the covers. Her hair spilled out over the pillows, and the sheet covered her naked body. She smiled. "Thank you. For everything."

"For rescuing a beautiful princess? How could I not?"

Her smiled faded. "Because you believe I betrayed you. I didn't, you know."

He nodded. "I know. For a while I didn't. I didn't trust myself to believe you, but when I was able to put aside my pride, I could see clearly again, and I knew. Deep down, I always knew." She extended her hand to him, and he took it, examining her long fingers as they wrapped around his. It was easier to talk if he didn't look at her. He cleared his throat. "I'm sorry I put you through all of this." She squeezed his fingers.

"Roshan, look at me." He looked up into warm, inviting eyes. "You didn't put me through anything. It was my brother and me behind all this. Not you. Never you."

He shook his head. "I should have made sure you didn't leave the palace. I knew your brother would do whatever he could to have you back."

"It was my decision to leave. I'm not the kind of person you can imprison to keep safe. That's not me."

He huffed a laugh. "No, I guess not."

There was a knock at the door, and a maid brought in hot tea, coffee, and snacks. Roshan rose from the bed. "I have to go now, but I'll be back." He took one last look at her, tucked up in bed, accepting a steaming mug of coffee from the maid and tore himself away. She'd be here when he returned. She wasn't going anywhere now. He'd make sure of that.

He thought she was asleep when he quietly entered the room much later, after having met with his irate ministers. He'd calmed them to some extent, and had made plans to ensure Shakira's safety, and had only then returned to her.

The lights were out, but as he approached, she turned

to him, her eyes wide, her expression anxious. "Is every-thing all right?"

He sat on the bed beside her. "I think it will be. There's nothing to worry about. You're safe here, and I've put plans in place to ensure that this doesn't escalate."

She sighed with relief. "Thank goodness."

"Can I get you anything?"

"You," she said simply.

"You have me. I'm not going anywhere. I don't trust anyone but me to look after you."

"That's good. But not good enough."

"What do you mean?"

"You're clothed, you're not in bed with me. I want you to make love to me, Roshan." He didn't move. "Please." Her voice sounded twisted as if caught in her throat, between wanting to say the word, and not wanting. The catch broke the spell.

He walked over to the bed and looked down at her. She would tempt a saint, and he was no saint. His Shakira had returned—strong, brave, and demanding what she wanted. It would have been churlish to refuse.

So he quickly undressed and got into bed beside her and made sure his lips warmed anywhere which needed to be warmed and anywhere that didn't. He kissed every inch of her quivering thighs as his fingers and lips explored her, readying her for when he buried himself deep inside of her.

She gasped and curled her legs around his hips. He thrust gently into her before drawing out slowly, and then thrusting once more into her and resting there, feeling the pulse of her and him combined.

He could watch her eyelashes fluttering against her

lids forever, he thought, as he slowly withdrew before easing back inside of her again. He reveled in how her wet warmth enveloped him, drawing him into her as if she had cast out a line and was reeling him in. And she'd got him—hook, line, and sinker.

She might have captured him, but he held the power at that moment, holding back his pleasure to give her what she wanted. It was only when he felt her breathing quicken, and she cried out his name and gripped his body tight against hers, that he allowed himself to come. His eyes narrowed as he watched her, and she watched him as his seed spilled deep into her. She was his now.

Roshan lay awake most of the night thinking through everything that had happened. He hadn't admitted everything to Shakira. He closed his eyes as the knowledge pressed down heavily that his actions, his affair with Shakira, had escalated tension to a point that was worse than it had been for decades. So much for a marriage, which would ease tensions. Instead, he was having an affair with the one woman he shouldn't—the one woman who was forbidden to him. How had he managed to make such a mess of things? But he knew.

Shakira made a soft noise and twisted in her sleep. As one arm flopped around his waist and she snuggled against him—her breathing coming smoothly once more as if his presence reassured her—he knew.

Shakira had come into his life with the full force of a jet engine, blasting everything else into oblivion. He stroked her hair until she fell into peaceful sleep again. He hadn't stood a chance.

CHAPTER 9

The next morning they made love again before Roshan reluctantly rose and showered, insisting Shakira remain in bed to rest. Despite her claims of being completely well, Shakira remained in bed because it was easier to watch Roshan as he went about his morning routine.

The time they'd spent together had been anything but routine, and now, in this domestic setting, it warmed her to the bottom of her heart to watch him. It helped her understand him. Behind his charm and smooth exterior, Roshan was a focused, disciplined, and clever man.

She understood him because he was very like herself. Trying to reconcile, from an early age, a life of high expectation and duty, against a desire for love and excitement—the duty balanced against the personal, always warring, always at odds. It created a tension that, at times, was unendurable. But, somehow now, because it was shared with him, it was endurable. It was even understandable.

Especially when he looked at her in that new way, which was both possessive and tender. During the previous night's lovemaking, they'd connected physically, emotionally, and mentally, as they'd never done before. And, she thought, as she stepped into the bathroom and turned on the shower, it made things a whole lot more complicated.

When she emerged, Roshan was on the phone in front of the window looking out to the sea, toward the misty land of Jazira. She stood beside him and followed his gaze. It was still her home in her heart, but it could never be her home again.

Roshan finished the phone call and turned to her. She could immediately see that something had happened.

"What is it?" she asked.

He gave her a glance which was designed to reassure but did nothing of the kind.

She pressed her lips together and shook her head. "Don't evade my question, Roshan. We need to tell each other the truth, we need to be open with each other. It's the only way. I need to know everything."

He nodded. "I'm meeting with Amir and Zavian in an hour."

She nodded. "Of course. You need to discuss what to do with me."

He took both her hands. "Listen to me, Shakira. We will not be discussing what to do with you. You're staying here with me. That is what will happen. That is not up for discussion. You are safe here, with me, and you must believe that."

He was a good and honorable man, and she knew that he believed what he said.

"You must know, Roshan, deep down, that I cannot stay here with you." She nodded to the misty horizon, which was clearing with each passing moment as the early morning mists burned off. "My being here will provoke my brother into action."

"That would not be sensible."

She smiled sadly. "I don't believe my brother has ever been accused of being sensible in his entire life." She swallowed. "I don't believe he's in his right mind anymore. The things I've heard him say, seen him do…" She shook her head. "He was always a weak man, but now he's not a sane one either. And those two things are dangerous. Especially for you if I'm here with you. I've angered him, and he wants me back."

"He will not get you back."

"No. And I will make sure of that."

"I won't let anyone harm you." She tried to pull away from his hands, but they were too firmly around hers. "I mean it, Shakira. This is too big for you to deal with on your own." He held up his hand to stop her from speaking. "I know you are strong, I know you want to handle this alone, but let me help."

She flung off his hands. "How can you help? Do you really think Amir and Zavian will approve of you helping me? They want you to marry Sheikha Elaheh, for goodness sake!"

He opened his mouth to speak but seemed to think better of it. She frowned. He was holding something back from her.

"What's happened?" She grabbed his hand. "You haven't told me everything, have you?"

"The Tawazun king."

Shakira nodded. "The sheikha's father. Yes?" She frowned. "What about him? Is he angry about what's happened? But why do I ask? Of course, he is. Both he and the sheikha must be furious about the increasing tension with my country."

"There's more."

"Yes? What?" She hardly dared utter the one-word questions.

"He's dead," he said quietly. "The King of Tawazun is dead."

She shook her head in disbelief. "Dead?"

"Of course we knew he was suffering from cancer, but he'd always looked so well, and had told us the treatment was going well. We understood that there was no imminent threat. It turned out the cancer had spread. He died suddenly. Asymptomatic. No one had any idea."

"Oh, my goodness! Poor Elaheh." She paused as she considered the implications which were massive. "Have the kings made plans to stabilize the situation?"

"It seems it's not necessary. The power vacuum we were afraid of isn't happening. Sheikha Elaheh has been pronounced Queen of Tawazun."

She sat down as if pushed, rubbed her forehead, and looked up at him with worried eyes. "Do you know how she feels about us? About what's happened? I hope it doesn't jeopardize your situation."

"She's agreed to meet with us."

This time Shakira swore under her breath. "Well, that must be a good sign, I guess?"

"We're taking it to be until we know for sure otherwise."

She stood up. "I should come also. I should front up."

"I don't think that's a good idea."

"It's time we put all our cards on the table. No more deception, no more secrets."

"It's too risky."

"It's too risky not to. Just picture it, you're all there, and she knows about me. Unless I see her and talk with her, she won't know if I'm a risk or not. None of them will know whether to believe you or not. For once and for all, we should address these issues directly."

Roshan rubbed his jaw in indecision. But Shakira had never been more sure of anything in all her life. Anything less than a united front would be dangerous.

"I'm no longer someone who can hide, Roshan."

He gave a faint smile and tucked her hair behind her ear. "*Habibti*, you never were." He kissed her and stepped away. "You must come, of course you must come. We are breaking new territory here, and you must be a part of it."

Shakira hadn't realized she was holding tension inside herself until he'd spoken. Only then did she blink and sigh with relief. Things had to change, and she had to change along with them. But there was one thing Roshan didn't know, and that was that, no matter what he wanted, no matter what they both felt, her destiny had altered forever. She was no longer an individual who was at the beck and call of her family. Her country needed her, and she would be there for it.

She would not be attending the meeting as Roshan's troublesome and forbidden lover, but as a princess of a country which needed her.

· · ·

SHAKIRA HAD NEVER BEEN to the desert fortress palace where all the three kings met, in the center of the old Havilah heartland. It was just as impressive as she'd imagined, with the addition of modern security she hadn't imagined.

As four helicopters came into land within minutes of each other, the drone and hum of the engines drowned the silence of the desert. The sand whipped up by the blades obscured the clarity of the mid-day desert light.

Roshan and Shakira had arrived first and were waiting in the ancient arched entrance for the others. Shakira glanced at Roshan, who stood, his feet astride, hands clasped before him, brilliant white robes billowing in the wind created by the helicopters. He looked more severe than she'd ever seen him before. He also looked more compelling. She could hardly reconcile this imposing man beside her with the man she knew in bed, who focused his complete attention on her. All eyes were on him, as the two kings, followed by Sheikha Elaheh—the new Queen of Tawazun—made their way toward them.

She'd seen Zavian and Amir before from a distance and felt a flutter of nerves as they strode across the courtyard toward them. They looked equally as stern and imposing as Roshan. They made their introductions before turning to watch the approach of the sheikha.

She walked ahead of a small contingent of ministers. She was much more petite than Shakira remembered. When she'd met her at the wedding, the sheikha's forceful character had made her seem larger than she actually was. With her erect posture and steady gaze, she was the epitome of dignity, despite her diminutive stature. While her contingent of ministers and assistants all wore sunglasses and continually shifted their gaze around the courtyard, checking security, her eyes were uncovered. They were almond-shaped and piercing as they looked from one man to the other, before resting briefly on her. She might be slight, but Shakira could sense the powerful spirit which resided in that small frame.

The men beside her seemed to sense it also. They greeted her with deference and, Shakira thought, something like embarrassment. After all, hadn't each of them been tasked with marrying her, only to fall in love with someone else and withdraw? And now here was Roshan, the last of them, with her, Shakira, the woman who could come between Elaheh and Roshan, and prevent a peace which they all needed now, more than at any other time.

"Welcome, Your Highness," said Roshan. "It is a great honor to have you join us at this critical time."

Elaheh nodded coolly, before exchanging stilted pleasantries with the Amir and Zavian. Then she turned to Shakira.

"We meet again, Princess. Except, of course, last time we didn't know your identity."

Shakira refused to be bested by this woman. "Unfortunately, I was not at liberty to disclose it. But I am pleased to be here today to rectify that situation."

Elaheh's eyes brightened with interest. "Perhaps our meeting today may be more constructive than I imagined."

"I hope so."

"We are living through a time of great change."

"A time of great opportunity, also," said Shakira.

"Maybe. I hope so. Although grief also comes with that change."

Shakira suddenly remembered that the only reason this woman was here, representing her country, was that her father had died. "Of course. May I offer my condolences on your father's passing?"

The steady strength in the sheikha's eyes flickered a little, revealing a glimpse of the woman behind the surface. Still, it was quickly covered, and the all-powerful royal, upon whose support the peace of the region depended, returned once more. "Thank you." She turned to the others. "Perhaps we should proceed. I don't have much time."

Shakira managed to prevent a smile as the three powerful kings did as the diminutive sheikha suggested, and they followed her into the boardroom.

Once seated, the sheikha held out a dainty be-ringed hand to quiet the men. They were immediately silenced. She turned to Shakira. "Why are you here?" she asked. Shakira, while taken aback, appreciated the directness.

"Our region is under stress. I am an enemy of my brother, the King of Jazira, and have become a friend of the King of Sharq Havilah."

The sheikha's serious face slowly moved to Roshan. "So I hear." Then she moved to the others, one by one, before settling first on Amir. "Each of you spurned my father's advances to marry me."

Amir shifted in his seat. "I apologize, Your Majesty. I meant no offense, but when I met the mother of my child again, well..." He petered out, unable to continue. It seemed he didn't have to.

"You fell in love." The word wasn't soft on her lips. She said it with something like disdain. She turned to Zavian.

"And then my father approached you." She placed a heavy emphasis on the last word.

"I, also, meant no offense, Your Majesty but—"

She held up her imperious hand once more, cutting Zavian quiet. "Spare me the details." Then she turned to Roshan. "And then you drew the short straw. Let down by your fellow kings, you had to put aside your womanizing ways"—Shakira felt Roshan blench at the description—"and marry me. But, instead, you take a lover."

Then she turned to Shakira, whose heart and stomach sank. She didn't think she'd ever met such a commanding woman as this sheikha, who could strike fear into the three kings. Shakira couldn't help but feel that if the sheikha had met any of the men before they'd fallen in love, they wouldn't have stood a chance but marry her, if the sheikha had wished it, of course.

"And then there's you. The woman who, it would seem, the famous womanizer has fallen for."

Shakira glanced at Roshan, who turned a slight shade of red and shot her back an uncomfortable glance.

"What is the matter, Roshan?" asked Elaheh. "Don't tell me that you've told your officials, but not the woman in question?" She gave the first hint of a smile that was quickly swallowed. "So, none of you three wish to marry me." They didn't know where to look. "And yet, you need my agreement for peace in our region."

The silence was deafening.

Elaheh rose and walked around the room, stopping from time to time at a portrait of their ancestors. Then she turned to them. "My father and I did not agree on everything."

Their collective hearts sank.

"But, Your Highness, who you will marry is of the utmost importance to the future peace and prosperity of all our nations," Roshan interjected.

She cast him an imperious glance. "We did not agree," she continued, as if she hadn't been interrupted, "on marriage. You see, gentlemen, when my father was alive, I would have done as he asked and married one of you. I had no preference." She shrugged. "You are all alike to me. But things have changed. My father is no longer alive, and I am in control of whether I marry—or not." She shot a fierce look around the men who sat as quietly as schoolboys. Shakira had to struggle not to laugh. But then the sheikha's gaze rested on her and any thought of laughing disappeared under her stern gaze.

"But," Elaheh continued. "Although my father is no longer with us, I share his desire for peace in this region, and I have every intention of securing it for all our countries' sakes. And I will do it single-handedly. After each of you has spurned marriage to me, I don't look favorably upon the institution. I do not need to marry, and I have no intention of marrying. Now, if that's quite clear, perhaps we can get down to business." She looked up at Shakira. "I assume you are on our side, now, Princess Shakira?"

Shakira nodded. Again the simplicity of the question was refreshing after so much deception. "I am. My father and my brother have steadily led my island nation away from the right path. Generations ago, we were a proud seafaring nation, but that degraded to pirating and violence. It needs to change again. My people are afraid, and so they should be because my brother is deteriorating." She swallowed. "He needs to be replaced. And there

are able men there to do it. I believe an uprising is imminent. I just hope it isn't bloody."

"Indeed. Then we have much to discuss." Elaheh raised
a cool eyebrow and focused on and released each one of
the kings in turn. They glanced away, uneasy under her
direct, confronting gaze.

There was something about this woman who was now
Queen of Tawazun, which Shakira admired. She was
strong, and it was obvious she was going to make the
three men pay for spurning her as a partner—king or no
king.

But, by the end of the meeting, it was clear that,
despite Roshan's arguments and her own assurances, the
others refused to take Shakira into their confidence. She
might be an ally, but she wasn't a trusted one yet. And she
had no option but to sit out most of the meeting.

She could hardly blame them. After all, she'd been sent
to spy on Roshan in the first place by her brother. The
kings couldn't be certain that she never had any intention
of carrying it out.

Roshan was quiet on the helicopter ride back to his
country. But when he reached the palace and jumped out
and held out a hand to help her out, he kept his hand on
her arm.

"We need to talk, Shakira."

She nodded. They walked in silence to his official suite
of rooms, and her heart sank. Official? It could only mean
one thing. She'd be leaving, forced back to Europe, away
from her lands and people.

"Drink?" he asked, walking towards the drinks cabinet.

"Yes, please. Something soft."

He poured himself a neat whiskey and a long soda

water for her. He sighed as he dropped some ice into her glass. Then he picked them up and turned to her, and she could see the torment and confusion in his face.

She placed her hand on his arm. "It's okay, you know. I hardly expected them to welcome me with open arms. Why should they?"

"Because I said they could trust you, that's why."

"Maybe they think that our"—she paused as she tried to think of the correct word—"relationship, might have impaired your judgment."

He swilled the amber liquid around his glass. "That's exactly what they think." He took a swig of his whiskey. "I was outvoted. I'm sorry."

She shrugged. "I didn't expect anything different. Just so long as you know that I'm not the enemy. You do, don't you?"

"You know I do. We can show them the truth, that you are trustworthy. Stay. I want you to stay here."

She blinked and looked away. She glanced out the window at the distant lights of her country. Where she should be. Where she couldn't be.

"How can you want me to stay here? I'll jeopardize everything."

"No, you won't. I know you won't."

"But you must see that it's not down to me. Simply my presence here will jeopardize everything. My brother won't rest until he gets revenge on you for helping me escape. Roshan, I'm trouble, and Zavian and Amir are correct. I can't stay anywhere near you, or their countries. I have to leave."

He gripped her arms. "We can make it work. I'm determined to. We can withstand anything your brother throws at us. I have the power, and my country will stand strong behind me. Zavian and Amir will also support us. I know they will."

"Just you saying that shows I must leave. I'm splitting you three up, and there's only strength in being strong together."

"I'll make it work," he said, between ground teeth. "I will. You must trust me."

"I do trust you, Roshan. That isn't the question. The person I don't trust is my brother. He could break your, Zavian's, and Amir and Elaheh's worlds apart because I'm here."

"I want you in my life, Shakira."

She shook her head. "Roshan, don't you see? That's the one thing you can't have." Tears threatened to choke her, but she refused to shed them. If she cried, she'd be in his arms, and then, they'd go to bed. That wouldn't solve anything. The only thing that would solve it all would be for her to be strong. Didn't she always pride herself on her strength?

She shook her head at him. "I'm sorry." Before he could reply, she'd run from the room and to her quarters. She'd stay the night, but she'd leave before sunrise. She had no choice. And she knew that Roshan also understood that, no matter what he said.

CHAPTER 10

Shakira awoke to the pale light of dawn. She blinked for a few moments as she tried to shed the traces of dreams and figure out where she was. Then she remembered—Roshan's palace at Sharq Havilah. She'd been awake until the early hours wondering if he'd come to her.

He hadn't. She'd hoped he wouldn't come; it would complicate things. She'd also hoped he would come because she was used to complicated. But he hadn't, and she had to live with that. And would have to for the rest of her life because she knew that they had no future together. She could no longer live in the region. She didn't belong to the lands of Havilah, and she was now an enemy in her own homeland of Jazira.

She raked back her hair, rose, and pulled on her robe. She padded softly to the window and flung it open wide. She needed the fresh air of morning to sweep away the cloudy vestiges of the deep sleep into which she'd eventually fallen.

The view from the palace was beautiful from any direction—taking in the old city and the sea and mountains—but from this particular window, it was especially poignant, for her at least. Because directly over the sea was the hazy island of Jazira. She gazed at it hungrily, trying to identify the jagged mountain interior in the dim light, the tumble of buildings around the palace, the busy port from where ships sailed to all corners of the world. But there was nothing but a hazy smudge on the horizon. She closed her eyes, and only then did she see all the elements of Jazira which she longed to see. She felt reassured because she knew after she left here that they would always be with her, long after she'd gone because go she must.

Her bags were already packed, not that she had much. Only the little with which she'd entered Sharq Havilah a few weeks earlier, but which seemed like a lifetime ago. The rest—the beautiful clothes and jewels which Roshan had given her—could stay. She wouldn't need them where she was going.

She wasted no further time in showering and dressing. She didn't return to look at the view. She had to be firm, and there was no strength to be had in wanting what you couldn't have.

She took one last look around the room where she'd both been treasured lover and prisoner, her heart full of emotion, before closing the door.

Her low-heeled soft-soled shoes made the barest whispering sound along the marble corridor. The gray light of pre-dawn gleamed through the upper windows, barely shedding light onto the shadowy corridor. It was only when she emerged into the domed ceiling hallway that she could see clearly. She paused and looked around at the richly decorated and grand room—beautiful in a way that was very different from her own ancient and less refined country.

She didn't want to bump into Roshan now. There was nothing to be said which hadn't already been said, nowhere they could go with their feelings. There was only one thing left, and that was for her to leave. She didn't trust herself with him. She'd never been able to resist him, even when she didn't know him.

She smiled at the memory of the first night she'd met him, in this very room, and at their instant animal attraction. She was suddenly flooded with desire for him and turned on her heels, and walked quickly to the door. There was no time for such indulgence. She had to leave before he found her and threatened her resolve.

Outside, the gardens had just been watered, and the air was full of moisture. The plants dripped and glistened in the soft, shadowy light. She would miss it—the heat of the day, the cool of the night, and the extremes of parched deserts and luxuriant oases. There was nothing like it, in this world, nor nothing like it in her heart. All these countries had once been one. Only her own had proved rogue and had been a thorn in the side of the other countries. She took one last breath of the scented air and turned to walk towards the exit. It was then that she saw him.

He was sitting under the shade of a tree on a plain stone bench by the door in the exterior wall through which she would have to leave. She didn't think he'd heard her because he looked unguarded. His elbows rested on his knees, and his hands were clasped tightly.

His head was bowed as if he were either half-asleep or his thoughts were miles away.

She paused mid-step, holding her breath, afraid to disturb him, not trusting either of them. But her doubts and fears were swept away by her emotions as she looked at him. She had never seen him look anything other than kingly, or masterful. But the word which came to her mind as he sat there was crushed. What could have brought this confident, assured, strong man to his knees?

She made no sound, and yet at that moment, he lifted his head suddenly and caught her gaze. He didn't move immediately but looked at her questioningly, as if scarcely able to believe it was her. She gripped her bag tighter and shuffled her feet, not sure where to go. She had thought she had escaped meeting him one last time. She'd been wrong.

As her movements registered, his gaze cleared, and he jumped up. His hands went to reach for her before he thrust them into the pockets of his trousers. His lips were pressed firmly together as if he didn't trust himself to speak first. His uncertainty was endearing. That, together with her first impression of him being crushed by something, was the only thing that made her do what she did. She stepped towards him, reached out, and touched his arm.

"Roshan, are you alright?" He shrugged but kept his hands firmly in his pockets. She narrowed her eyes as she took in the shadows beneath eyes which were weary and blood-shot. "Have you even slept?"

He shrugged again and shook his head distractedly. "I was too busy."

"Busy? What were you doing?" Thoughts of war,

economic collapse, death—each and every one of the disasters that could fell a man—swept through her mind. "Please, tell me."

He frowned. "What was I doing? Thinking. About you, and about me. About how I don't want you to leave."

She swallowed and blinked back her tears. Instinctively she reached out to him, and he needed no further invitation. He gripped her hand within both of his and kissed it.

"Oh, Roshan," she sighed, as he lifted his head from her fist and kissed her on the lips instead. She could no more resist him than not breathe.

Any thought of him feeling crushed was swept away by the way he kissed her. He was back to his commanding self, exploring her lips, mouth, and tongue with a sensuality which turned her legs to jelly and her mind to mush. She tilted her head back, opening her mouth for him to take whatever he wanted from her. He groaned inside her, and his hands slid over her back before settling on her behind, pulling her hard against him so she could feel how ready he was for her.

He had total control of her now, but it was he who finally pulled away. He nuzzled her neck, whispering endearments, before pulling her tight in his arms and holding her fiercely as if he didn't want ever to let her go.

Finally, he pulled away, and held her head in his hands, but his expression was fierce as if he'd come to some kind of decision.

"I could have you here and now, Shakira. You always do this to me."

"Then take me, Roshan, because my need for you is too great. I want you more than anything."

He drew in a harsh breath and shook his head. "No," he ground out. "I won't. My passion for you stops me from thinking clearly, but I must think now. Our future depends upon it."

She tried to shake her head to deny his words of sense which she didn't want to hear, but he held her head firmly between his hands. "Shakira, I love you, but what I don't know is if you love me."

She caught her breath in her throat. She'd wondered what had affected him when she'd first seen him. She'd thought something must have happened, but she'd forgotten the one thing which made people suffer above everything else, which they sought their whole lives, which gave meaning to life—love.

She hadn't known for sure until that moment that he loved her as much as she loved him. Not that she'd told him that. And she couldn't now, not without complicating what she was about to do, because love didn't change a thing. It only made everything that much harder. And she couldn't do that to him.

Despite that, she hesitated, enjoying that moment when all the possibilities in the world hung in balance between them—life could still go one way or another. She'd heard people talking about the crossroads of life where you choose one road or another and have to live with the consequences for the rest of your life. And this was one such. She knew that the course of her life depended on this conversation, whichever way it might go.

"Shakira," he repeated. "Will you stay?"

She shook her head, tiny little shakes as she tried to reconcile what she should say, with what she wanted to say and do. She sucked in a sharp breath. "There's no point."

He took a step toward her. "There's every point." He lifted her chin to the light. "That's better. I can see your face more clearly now." He gave a small smile that was swiftly gone. "You can never hide your thoughts or feelings. They flit across your face like shadows chasing the sun."

She tried to smile, but nothing happened. Sadness got you like that sometimes, and she suddenly knew what she had to do. "Then I think I'm in for a rainy season."

He dropped his hand. "And that's what you choose?"

"It is."

He grimaced but nodded in acceptance at his words. "I need to know one thing, Shakira. Is it only for political reasons?"

She shook her head. "I've been pushed and pulled and manipulated my whole life, Roshan. As a man, a sheikh and a king, I doubt you'll understand what it's like. But from the moment I was born, I was used as a pawn—first between my parents as they chose me as their battleground—and then politically, as my father, followed by my brother, tried to force me to marry first one man and then another. And I'm still here—at the center of a web of intrigue created by men, for men." She shook her head. "I'm tired of it, Roshan. I'm sorry, but I need to take control of my own life for once. No matter what..." She couldn't continue, a sob lodged in her throat, and she knew that it wouldn't be fair for her to say what was in her heart. What was in her head was sufficient.

He shook his head as his frown lowered, leaving the lower part of his face in shadow while his forehead and eyes were bathed in the first raspberry rays of sunshine, the color of blood.

Then he sucked in a breath and cleared his throat. "You're a strong woman, Shakira. Don't ever forget that. You were raised in a chauvinistic family, and you deserve time to find your independence. I do understand. I don't know how, but I do. And you should do exactly as you say."

"Oh," she said, suddenly deflated. She'd taken that left fork in the road which her mind had told her to do, and which she knew she had to do, but there was a part of her —larger than she'd supposed—which hoped he'd refuse to let her go. But that was stupid. Did she really want him to take hold of her, throw her over his shoulders, tighten his grip around her hips and take her back to his room and keep her there, making love to her until she agreed to stay?

The answer shouldn't have been yes.

He stepped to one side. "I wish you all the best in the world, Shakira. I mean that. You're a wonderful woman, and you deserve a wonderful life, not a life where you're tossed around by men to meet their own needs."

Tears glossed her eyes. She swallowed.

"And, if you ever change your mind," he continued, "I'm here for you."

She gave a choked laugh. "You'll be long married by then, Roshan."

He shook his head. "No. No, I won't. I have an excellent reason not to."

"I've put you off women?" she said, trying to wipe that serious expression from his face, an expression which scared her because of its emotional intensity. It scared her because it threatened to break through the flimsy barrier, which was the only thing propelling her forward to a future her intellect was telling her was what she needed.

Self-preservation. It had ways of looking after you when all you wanted to do was run into your lover's arms and bury your nose and lips and eyes into his bare chest.

"I guess you could put it like that."

He stepped away, and she watched him turn and walk back inside the palace. She stayed until the red glow of the rising sun rose above the wall and showered the courtyard garden in deep orange light. A bird rose from the trees and burst into song. Spiders' webs sparkled, damp with the early morning watering, and the water shimmered as if welcoming the sunlight with a purr of delight. Everything was normal, everything was beautiful, just as it always was. Except he was gone, and the light inside of her had gone out with him.

ROSHAN DIDN'T LOOK BACK. He couldn't bear to see her beautiful face, full of indecision overlying a fundamental strength which was impressive.

He'd lain awake all night working out how he could tell her that he wanted her to stay, that they were simply two people, two ordinary people who had a right to be together. He'd lain awake, working out the words he needed to persuade her to stay. But he'd done none of those things. All he'd done was tell her to leave because he knew that that was what she needed to do. Was that what love was about, he wondered as he returned to begin his day as king of a country he was starting to resent.

Yes, there was a reason why he would never marry

anyone else, but there was no point in telling her the real reason. Let her think she'd put him off women for life. In a way, she had. Because there was only one woman in his life from now on, but it seemed he couldn't have her because she needed what he couldn't give her. Independence.

By mid-morning Roshan was busy at work with his ministers. He was sitting back in his chair, trying to focus on a presentation a junior minister was giving on urban development of his city when his assistant burst into the room and locked eyes with him. A dagger-thrust of unease slew through him.

He rose and indicated that the others should continue without him, and his assistant handed him a sheet of roughly torn paper which had been seized from the printer in a rush.

He had to read it twice. He nodded grimly to his assistant. "Inform Cabinet." Then he went back to his desk and held up his hand to interrupt the presentation. "News from Jazira!" He took a breath to calm his pounding heart. "The king has been assassinated." There were gasps around the room, and he held up his hand once more to quiet them. "It seems there has been a coup, and the military has taken control."

"What is it they want? War?"

"I don't know if they want war, but what I do know is that they want a new ruler."

"Who?" asked one of the men.

"The one remaining member of the royal family. Sheikha Shakira of Jazira."

All eyes were fixed on him. It was widely known that Shakira had been a constant visitor at the palace and in his quarters and that the two were close.

"Did you know?" asked one of the men hesitantly.

It would be what everyone wondered, Roshan thought, despite irritation that he'd have to respond. He knew he had no choice. "I had no idea."

"Did she?"

"Again, I have no idea." His words emerged clipped between his lips. He could barely contemplate the idea that she'd known about the coup. How could she not? After all, she'd been imprisoned by the very guards who were now in charge. But even as the thoughts flitted through his mind, he knew that she had no idea that such a move by her supporters was imminent. "Get the other kings online. We need to talk urgently."

As he left the room to talk with the other kings about this development and how they would respond, Roshan couldn't help hoping that Shakira didn't have any idea. Because if she did, she'd been playing him as hard as she'd been played by men. Who was the fool who'd been manipulated now? Because, if she'd known about the assassination attempt, it surely wasn't her.

CHAPTER 11

The CNN newsflash screened just before Shakira's plane landed in London. She sat in horror as she watched the Jaziran army commander announce that the king had been killed in an uprising and had posthumously been denounced for crimes against his country and that the military had formed an interim government. Interim? Until what? Who did they intend would take control?

As soon as she got off the flight, she was ushered into the First Class Lounge—apparently upon instructions from the new Jaziran government—and they immediately made contact with her.

She sat, stunned, as she listened to the army's commander—a general who had been a soldier under her grandfather's reign, and a commander under her father's. It seemed her brother's reign had been the final straw—an outrage against the country's honor. She couldn't help but think Roshan would dispute that Jazira had any honor, but she knew differently.

But her shock only deepened when the conversation took a turn she hadn't foreseen, and he asked her to return and head the country.

She stared at the phone for a moment before replacing it against her ear. "You want me…" She trailed off, unable to voice the words which sounded so strange to her.

"To replace your brother, as sheikha of the family and Queen of Jazira. It must be you, my Princess. Only you have the power to evoke loyalty in the population amongst both those dissatisfied with your brother's corrupt reign and those loyal to the monarchy. You must return, my Princess; you must take your rightful place as monarch of Jazira."

Shakira let the line crackle and the silence lengthen between them. She felt at once a great loss and a fateful finality. She had no choice. It seemed the life of freedom she'd been seeking would never be hers. If she declined the throne of Jazira, she'd be condemning the people and country she loved to a life of uncertainty and struggle.

"Yes," she said softly. Her voice was hoarse, and she cleared her throat. "Yes," she said, more forcefully this time. "I will return and take my brother's place."

There was a soft grunt and sigh as if the minister had been holding his breath as he awaited her response. The relief was palpable.

"Thank you. It won't be easy, but you have the full support of the army and your ministers, as well as the people. You'll be welcomed with open arms."

"Right," she said, nodding as she tried to absorb what was about to happen to her. "Right. Thank you. I'll do my best to live up to your confidence in me."

"I have no qualms on that matter." The man's voice

softened. "Most of us have known you since you were a babe in arms, and we've recognized your integrity and wisdom which your grandfather also had. We know we will be safe in your hands."

She smiled into the phone as memories of the years growing up surrounded by this man and others like him flooded her mind. "We are all family together. We will make it through this turn of events and make Jazira great again. But on our own terms."

"We will, my Princess. But a word of caution. The notion of marriage will arise, and this has to be dealt with carefully. Nothing must be done to jeopardize the current delicate state of affairs."

She knew what he meant. "You're referring to the king of Sharq Havilah… to Roshan."

He cleared his throat. "There have been… rumors."

She didn't confirm or deny.

"And I can tell you that marriage to the king of Sharq Havilah would not be acceptable to our people."

She hesitated only a moment because she knew he was correct. "Of course," she said quickly. She felt the blow viscerally. She'd walked away from Roshan because her presence in Sharq Havilah jeopardized peace in the region and also to find her independence. Now, she had no choice but to return to Jazira and accept a role that would permanently divide her from him. "Of course," she repeated, more slowly this time.

She listened as the arrangements for her return to Jazira were described—a private plane, which was readying itself on the tarmac in London as they spoke—and what would happen over the next few days. She struggled against the feeling that she was once more on someone else's tracks, subject to someone else's whims and desires. But then she pulled herself up. In the short term, these people would guide her, but in the long term? It would be down to her. For the first time in her life, she saw a future in which she called the shots. The idea was both daunting and exhilarating.

"I'll see you this evening then."

"And then our work will begin." He paused. "Thank you, my Princess. You have done Jazira and its people a great kindness in taking on this role. Without you..." He trailed off.

"I know. And I don't want chaos and bloodshed. We've seen enough of that during my brother's and father's reigns. I have a very different vision."

"One that we all share, my Princess."

Shakira finished the call and looked around. The general must have either been confident or desperate because there were already people waiting for her to take her to the private jet. She approached them, and they all bowed.

"Your Highness," they greeted her. She guessed she'd have to get used to that.

IT HAD BEEN two months since Shakira had returned to Jazira and become its queen. Two months in which Roshan had watched Shakira grow into the role. He wasn't surprised she was so good at it. He knew she'd needed only two things—the support of her people, and time to develop confidence in her abilities. The former had been immediate, and the latter had taken less time than he'd thought.

The three kings and Elaheh, the Queen of Tawazun, waited in the shade of the desert fortress for the arrival of Shakira, the Queen of Jazira. Elaheh stood slightly to one side, still cool toward the others, their spurning of her not forgotten. As the distant throbbing of the helicopter grew louder, Roshan felt a stirring of excitement at the thought of seeing Shakira again, if in very different circumstances.

He couldn't help remembering the last time they'd been there and how different her status had been. Then, she'd been an inconvenience to the others and a forbidden lover to him. Now, she was the hope of the future to the others, and, he hoped, less forbidden to him. Especially if the talks about their region went well. And he didn't have any reason to think they wouldn't.

Shakira stepped out of the helicopter, waving away a hand to help her, and strode over to the kings and queen, her robes billowing in the blast of the helicopter rotors. She first went to Elaheh, and they greeted each other warmly. Then she approached Amir, Zavian, and finally, Roshan.

"Roshan," she said, dropping the formality she'd used with the others. It gave him hope.

"Shakira, it's good to see you." He bowed as the others had done.

"And you, too." She stepped away, looked at the others, and the intimacy suddenly vanished. Roshan wasn't in the presence of the old Shakira, but a queen who knew her responsibilities. It would make what he wanted harder, but not impossible.

"Let's go inside, we have much to discuss," he said, as

the kings stood to one side to allow Shakira and Elaheh to enter the ancient building.

When the two women had first met, Roshan had noticed that, despite the obvious tension which existed due to his and Shakira's relationship, Shakira and Elaheh had immediately taken to each other. During the past few months, Shakira and Elaheh had evidently built on their initial rapport because they were positively warm to each other now, almost to the exclusion of the three kings. Roshan had to suppress a wry smile when he saw Zavian's and Amir's frowning faces. None of them were accustomed to being upstaged by women, but he guessed it wouldn't hurt them.

They took their seats around the table, which, only months earlier, had been the sole province of the three kings, and Zavian took control of the meeting.

"Welcome, everyone, and thank you for coming."

Elaheh nodded haughtily and fixed her unsmiling gaze on Zavian. Shakira adjusted her robes and sat back in her chair at ease, and sensual still in her authority.

"I think I speak for both Elaheh and myself when I say we are glad to be here," said Shakira.

Elaheh nodded. "Indeed. Shakira and I have regularly met to put practical steps into place that will ensure closer cooperation between our countries."

Roshan could see that both Zavian and Amir were surprised by this news. He wasn't, though. It was just like Shakira to reach out to the only other woman ruler in the region and work closely with her. They were both women in a man's world and needed each other's support. He wished Shakira had reached out to him, but he knew it to be impossible.

"Stepping stones which are already bearing fruit," Roshan said. "I hope that we can work out similar connections in the treaty under discussion. Such a treaty between our countries can only benefit us all, can only make us stronger as a region, and a force to be reckoned with, both economically and politically, by the whole world."

"These are lofty goals, Roshan," said Shakira, the warmth in her eyes flaring as she met his gaze. "But not unachievable ones, I believe."

"This is what I also believe, Shakira," said Roshan, his voice lowering instinctively, as if there were no one else in the room. "Lofty goals are the only ones worth pursuing, the only ones of value." Her answering expression filled him with hope that the goals he had in mind would be achieved. But he knew it wouldn't be easy.

The moment was broken as Zavian cleared his throat. "Then I suggest we make a start." He nodded to an assistant who placed one sheet of paper before each of them. "Before you are the main points of the treaty. If we can agree on these by the end of this meeting, then the unachievable may, indeed, be achieved."

Roshan reeled in his thoughts and feelings. Now wasn't the time for them. Now was the time for work that would bring their countries together. And he, for one, had more than a vested interest in doing that.

THE TALKS LASTED all day because, as Amir had said, there had been much to discuss. It was the first time that all five countries had come together with the goal of ensuring peace and prosperity for all their lands. It seemed all it had needed was five rulers to want the same things—not to follow their own personal agenda, but to put their people and their countries first. By the end of the day, a peace treaty was signed, and more practical agreements on trade agreed.

"You will stay for dinner?" Roshan asked them all, but his gaze rested on Shakira, who was accepting a glass of iced water from the maid. "It would allow us to discuss matters in a more informal setting."

Elaheh—encouraged by the meeting and her former rancor with the three kings forgotten, or, at least, now hidden—agreed, as did Amir and Zavian. But when all eyes turned to Shakira, Roshan's heart fell.

She took a sip of her water, carefully placed it on the table, and fixed her scarf. She was the picture of composure and control, but her movements were still fluid and sensual, despite that. Roshan hadn't thought she could become more alluring, but it seemed her increased personal confidence and power had done just that.

"I cannot, I'm afraid." She licked her lips and looked around each one of them before her gaze rested on Roshan. "I must return to Jazira. I'm expected tonight."

"That is a shame. It would have been nice…" He trailed off as a lump unexpectedly rose into his throat. He blinked, and suddenly aware that all eyes were on him, summoned up some shred of conversation from the confusion of feelings that filled him. "It would have been nice to have found a little more about…" He sucked in a calming breath, "about"—he nodded, trying to give the emerging words, whatever they would be, emphasis and validity—"how your country is adjusting to the new regime." There was a long silence as if everyone knew that wasn't what he wanted to say. "How *you* are adjusting to the new regime."

There, it was out. He was only interested in Shakira, and how she was doing, and the tension in the atmosphere relaxed as if sensing that Roshan had finally said what he wanted to say. Amir turned to Elaheh and said something which Roshan couldn't hear, and had no interest in besides. He was simply relieved not to have the others bear witness to his fumbling speech and feelings.

"I think you know, Roshan," answered Shakira quietly. "I think you can see," she added.

He shot her a quick smile, which rapidly faded at her quiet tone. There was nothing hopeful to be found there. "You are adjusting well, Shakira. I am pleased. More than pleased."

Her smile lit up her face. "I knew you would be. You always wanted the best for me."

"I'm pleased you know that, for it's true."

"I do know that. And I'm grateful that I have such a true friend."

"Friend?" The word stuck in his throat. But, at that moment, Elaheh said something to Shakira. He had no time to question her on that description of their relationship—too weak, far too weak, an epithet to encompass what she meant to him. And if that was how she felt for him? Well, then, his unachievable goals might well stay that—unachievable.

As Roshan watched Shakira say her goodbyes to the others, he tried hard to check the chaos of emotions that threatened his composure. He tried to be the Roshan of old—charming, cynical, humorous—but could find nothing to say that fitted the bill. All he could think about was Shakira, his beautiful, sensual love, who was about to leave him without a further thought.

Eventually, she stood to one side. "I must leave now. But I thank you all for a successful day and look forward to our next meeting."

As Elaheh and Shakira embraced, the two kings eyed Roshan with a frown. They knew him well enough to understand what was going on. It was now or never. Roshan held the door open for Shakira.

"Please, allow me to escort you out," said Roshan. The others exchanged glances but didn't contradict Roshan. It was obvious he wanted some time alone with Shakira, and he didn't care who knew. Time was running out. Shakira held his gaze and then apparently made a decision. She nodded. She turned and farewelled the others, then walked ahead of Roshan out to the empty, echoing vaulted hallway.

He stopped by the door, in a corner, under a columned arch. "Shakira," he said quietly. She stopped dead in her tracks. Then he saw her shoulders heave and relax and she turned to him. The look in her eyes reassured him. This was his Shakira of old.

"The way you say my name," she said, with that gorgeous husky voice of hers. "It's not like any other. No one says it as you do."

"I'm glad. I wouldn't want anyone else to have the same feeling for you as I do when I say your name."

She blushed, and he nearly went to her. Instead, he balled his hands into fists to stop himself. This was too important.

"You're looking well, Shakira." He conjured a smile from somewhere deep inside. "Being queen suits you."

She answered his smile. "I'm what I always wanted to be—in control. But, more than that, I feel happy for the first time in my country. We're finding peace, and my people are happier than they have been since my grandfather was on the throne. Things are looking good for Jazira, Roshan."

"And for all of us because of it. We have a lot to thank you for."

"You and the other kings' help has proved a decisive factor in our stability. And for that, I have to thank you all."

"And what about the future? Your future."

"My future," she replied, frowning. "My people are still suspicious of Havilah's three kingdoms, and it will take time for us to move forward with this treaty."

"But in time?" he asked, his stomach sinking.

"In time?" she shrugged. "In time, I'll be married, no doubt. That is what my advisors have in mind for me anyway."

"Marriage. It is a good idea." His spirits lifted again. "Do you have anyone in mind?"

Her steady gaze didn't leave his. "My ministers do. My prospective husbands are all from Jazira. Apparently, no one else will do. If I marry an outsider, people will be suspicious that the person will want to seize power from me. A Jaziran noble is the only option. Someone who has no other interests outside of Jazira."

All words and thoughts evaporated from Roshan's mind. His hopes for the future vanished in a puff of smoke, extinguished by her words. He opened his mouth to speak, but no words came.

"What was it you wanted to see me about, Roshan? I'm sorry, I shouldn't have interrupted."

He shook his head, and it was the hardest thing he'd ever done. "Nothing. I simply wanted to make sure you were okay with everything that has happened."

"I am, thank you."

He watched her walk toward the waiting helicopter, every fiber of his being deadened, numbed by pain. He refused to allow the feelings to surface. There would be time for that later. Instead, he watched the helicopter take off, aware that she wasn't looking toward him but straight ahead, as if he'd ceased to exist. He watched until his eyes were wet, watering under the harsh sunlight. Yes, it was definitely the harsh sunlight.

SHAKIRA DIDN'T ALLOW herself to look toward him. Instead, she looked straight ahead. But she felt his gaze grazing her cheek nonetheless. She forced herself to be pleased that everything had gone according to plan. She'd known he would try to see if there was any future between them—what they had was too powerful and enduring to ignore. She certainly hadn't been ignoring it. How could you ignore anything that intense?

No, what had been occupying her mind was how to minimize the pain for him. She didn't mind taking it on herself. It was part of the duty which had befallen her. But she loved Roshan too much to drag him through uncertainty and misplaced hopes. She'd had to be hard and make him believe she felt nothing for him, make him think that what they'd experienced had been transitory, fleeting, something which hadn't endured. It was a lie. Of course it was. But it would have been worse for him if she'd told him the truth—that she loved him. Now, all he had to contend with was a broken heart and the belief that he'd misjudged her and her feelings for him. It would be easier that way.

Suddenly pain filled her, and she twisted around in her seat and looked at the dwindling dot that was Roshan, who had just turned to go inside. She turned around in her chair abruptly.

"Is everything all right, Your Highness?" asked the Air Steward.

She nodded and blew her nose. "Just some sand in my eyes, I think."

CHAPTER 12

"I don't see what's so important that I need to cut my holiday short," Xander grumbled, checking his phone once more before accepting a coffee from the maid, with a winning smile.

No doubt about it, Roshan thought, his little brother had spent too much of his youth modeling himself on him. Their mother had always said as much, and now he could see the evidence for himself. His little brother had become the playboy he'd always wanted to be. Except there was one big difference between them—Xander had no interest in duty. And it was about time he did.

"Cut your holiday short?" Roshan snorted and perched on the windowsill overlooking his city, his arms folded as he inspected his little brother. "You spend more time on holiday than anyone else I know."

Xander shot him a winning smile, and Roshan, like everyone else, relented a little. It was impossible not to when subjected to his little brother's charm offensive. "But you have to admit I work hard too."

Roshan scoffed, unable to be angry at his brother. "Work?" He rose and walked over to the desk and indicated the neat piles of stacked papers. "This is work. Not your dilettante business doing…" He hesitated, as he was never quite sure what his brother did. "Whatever it is that you do."

Xander glanced at the desk. "Haven't your staff moved into the electronic age?"

"Some of them, but by no means all, despite my requests." He sat at the desk and steepled his fingers, tapping his lips thoughtfully. "But maybe you could make inroads there."

Xander's eyebrows shot up. "Me? Why would I want to do that?"

"You're always telling me that you know how to run businesses. This is an international business. You could help me run it."

Roshan would have laughed at his brother's face if his response hadn't been so important to him.

"It's nothing like!" spluttered Xander.

Roshan leaned forward, his elbows on the desk observing his brother. "It's exactly like. It's all about cash flow, investments, people, morale, culture, competition. What?" He couldn't help smiling. "Aren't you up for the challenge? You? The man who reputedly never shies away from one?"

"What the hell are you talking about, Roshan? You've never wanted my help ruling Sharq Havilah. Ever since Father died, you've taken over and loved it. Don't tell me you want to take up some hobbies and need more time, because I won't believe you."

"Hobbies," Roshan murmured. "I guess you could call it a new-found hobby. I'm serious."

Xander flopped down into a chair, his eyes wide. "You're serious!"

Roshan nodded. "I've never been more serious. I need your help, Xander. Something's happened which has made my ruling of Sharq Havilah untenable."

"Untenable," he repeated, incredulous.

Roshan smiled. "You must be thrown if you keep repeating my words. Yes, I'm serious about the need for your return to Sharq Havilah. You see, I can't continue as king. And I want you to take my place."

Roshan didn't think there was anything else he could have said, which would have made Xander at a loss for words. He'd never seen him so stunned.

"Since Jazira and Tawazun have both been taken over by the sheikhas of those countries, our country has never been stronger," Roshan continue. "There's nothing wrong there. Amir, Zavian, and I work well together, and all five of us have plans for furthering our ties."

"So..." Xander said. "Let me get this straight. Everything is working well in the 'business world' of Sharq Havilah. We have peace, no imminent threats to our countries, you're well, and you've never shown any inclination to live elsewhere. So what the hell is going on? Why all this talk of me taking over from you? Not that I would. The idea is absurd!"

Roshan tapped his fingers on the desk. "It's not absurd at all. Your business acumen is far superior to mine."

"That's true. Your strengths have always been with women." Xander smiled, but then his smile faded, and he leaned forward. "That's it, isn't it? There must be women involved. That's always been your weakness."

Roshan winced at his brother's accurate assessment of the situation. "Woman," he corrected. "One woman."

Xander swore under his breath and leaned back in his chair once more, his eyes never leaving Roshan's, as if he could reach into his mind and extract the truth. It made Roshan uncomfortable because Xander always had had a gift for understanding people. "One woman."

"There you go again, repeating what I say." Roshan jumped up and strode to the window and looked out, turning his back on Xander, needing to keep some of his thoughts secret at least. "Yes, one woman," he confirmed, without looking back at his perspicacious brother.

Xander swore again. "You must have it bad, brother."

Roshan heard Xander scrape back the chair and come and stand beside him. He didn't try to look at Roshan, but joined him in surveying the city over which the rich light of sunset was spreading. To the right, the city disappeared into a haze beyond which lay the mountains and the land of Tawazun which had once been joined to theirs.

"I have. I love her. I'm in love. I'm besotted. She's the only one for me. Ever."

Xander let out a slow whistle and nodded. "Okay. So I believe you. It's serious. So, what's the problem. Is she married?"

"No. She's not married."

"So… doesn't she like the idea of becoming queen of Sharq Havilah? I'd have thought most women would give their right arm to marry someone like you—rich, powerful, and handsome, although not as handsome as his younger brother, admittedly."

Roshan shook his head at his brother's claim. "She's not most women."

"So what did she say when you asked her to marry you."

Roshan didn't answer immediately. Then he sighed. "I haven't asked her."

Xander threw his hands in the air. "Then what is this all about? Ask her to marry you, she'll say yes, and then we can all live happily ever after—with me, a thousand miles from here!"

"I know for a fact that she won't marry me if I'm king."

"How can you know that? What has she got against being a queen, for goodness sake?"

"Nothing."

"You're talking in riddles."

Roshan sighed. "She doesn't want to be queen of Sharq Havilah because she's already a queen."

Again, it appeared he'd silenced his usually talkative younger brother, who just turned and stared at him. Eventually, he shook his head. "You're incredible. You could have any woman in the world—and probably have if half the gossip is true—and you've chosen a queen. Who is she?"

"Shakira, queen of Jazira."

Xander closed his eyes at the news and grimaced. He drew a deep breath and opened his eyes. "A Jaziran Sheikha. The only known enemy to us and our country."

"An enemy no longer, thanks to Shakira."

Xander shook his head. "So you wish to abdicate, hand the crown to me, and make an honest woman of her?"

Roshan nodded. "That's basically the idea."

"And what if she refuses? What if she simply doesn't

want to marry you because you're you, not because you're king. You must have thought of that."

Roshan stuck out his chin stubbornly. Of course he'd thought of that, but he wasn't about to voice his fears to his little brother. "She'll marry me. I know how she feels."

"And how do you know that? Did she tell you?"

"Not in so many words."

Again Xander swore and called Roshan a name.

"You know I'm not stupid, and you know our parents were married," he replied mildly. "I know her, Xander." This time he met his brother's gaze directly in an attempt to convey the one thing he knew and trusted beyond anything else. "We were meant to be together. I love her, and I know"—he tapped his heart—"that she loves me."

"Then why hasn't she told you?"

"Because she knows our present situation precludes a relationship between us, and she would never ask me to abdicate."

Again, his brother's laser eyes searched his own, but this time he didn't flinch. He had nothing to hide and everything to gain by his brother's understanding of him. The seconds lengthened until Xander nodded his head slowly.

"You do believe what you say, and I've never known you to get things wrong. It's always been one of your more irritating qualities." Xander shrugged and looked back at the view, his gaze losing its focus as his thoughts turned inward. For all his brother's bravado, he was a deep thinker, and, deep down, he knew he'd do the right thing. Family and blood won over everything.

Roshan was aware of the cooling evening breeze springing up off the sea, bringing its salt-edged freshness with it. His mouth grew dry and his heart thudded. As each second passed, the fear grew tighter in his throat. But he'd wait for his brother to speak if it killed him.

"Okay," Xander said, turning to Roshan and extending a hand. "I'll take it on so you can go on your fool's errand. But if I come here, if I give up everything I have, the life I've made overseas, to return and take over from you, you need to know that it's final. I won't be going back. I won't be returning the kingship to you if your life turns to dust. That's my offer. All or nothing."

Relief swept through Roshan. He took Xander's extended hand, and they shook. Then he pulled his brother to him and embraced him. "Thank you."

"You owe me, brother. I can't think why the hell I'm doing this, giving everything up for you and your country."

"Our country," corrected Roshan.

Xander nodded. "Yes, I thought I could leave, but I guess its tight hold has remained somewhere deep inside."

"It's called your heart."

Xander scoffed. "We weren't raised to think of our hearts, and I haven't managed to locate mine yet. Unlike you."

They stood uncertainly for a few moments. Roshan knew that from that point on, both their lives would take different turns, and neither knew what lay ahead. "I truly hope the same happens to you."

"Right," said Xander, patently not believing him. "I'd best go and cancel my life." He grunted and shook his head. "I can't believe I've just said that."

Roshan laughed. "Nor can I, but I'm more than happy you have."

Xander grimaced. "I must be mad."

Roshan knew that the decision hadn't been as easy as Xander had made it look and that the next few months or years would be hard for him. "You're not mad. You're my brother, and I love you. And I'll be here to help, in the background," he added. "I'll be, or do, anything you want, so long as I can marry Shakira."

Again Xander nodded. "Well, if I'm not mad"—he headed for the door—"then you probably are." It was the last thing he said before closing the door.

Roshan ignored him and tossed his phone in the air, caught it, and selected a contact. "Organize a boat to take me to Jazira in one week's time."

THE CABINET MEETING was drawing to a close, and Shakira was exhausted. She wondered when the work would let up. It was constant, and she felt isolated and lonely, despite the support of her advisors.

"There's one more item. The Havilah Sha'ab reef. It's long been a bone of contention between Sharq Havilah and Jazira. They want access to the whole thing."

Shakira's senses awoke abruptly at the name of Sharq Havilah. "Fine," she said quietly, as she remembered that day swimming with Roshan near the reef, unable to go on it, and all that had meant for Roshan and his people.

The cabinet all looked suddenly at Shakira. "But… but we can't," spluttered her advisor.

"Why not?"

"Because blood has been spilt over that reef. It was a hard battle to gain it all."

"It wasn't ours to begin with," she said mildly. "The least we can do is share it." Then she remembered the look of love on Roshan's face that day on the beach, and it was like a dagger thrust deep inside her, drawing blood. And she knew she'd never be able to stem that bleeding because she could never have that love. It was forbidden. Her country needed her, and it refused to have him. She had no choice.

She lifted her chin defiantly, drawing all her strength to meet the official's eye. "We will share the reef. Our job is to move forward into a future of peace. This is simply one small step to symbolize that."

The officials were beginning to understand the strength of her personality now. She was no longer the woman who was continually manipulated by men. She called all the shots now, and everyone did as she commanded. They had no choice; the people loved and wanted her. She held all the power.

"It will be done."

She nodded, and they bowed and left the room. The vast chamber was empty now except for her. She gripped the armrests of her chair and rose, relieved to find the shakiness which had beset her at the memory of Roshan, and the reef, had disappeared back deep inside of her. She walked to the door and opened it onto the busy corridor of people, to all intents and purpose a strong and decisive ruler once more.

No one would ever know what was going on in her heart, but she would always know. She just hoped that one day she'd wake up to find the sharp pain of loss had reduced to a dull ache.

"Ambassador." She greeted the first man lined up to

meet her. She conversed with him as if all was normal. And she hoped one day it would be.

ROSHAN DECIDED ARRIVING incognito would be best. He didn't want her officials making a big thing of it—what he wanted to do needed quiet, subtlety, privacy. He wouldn't get that if he arrived in his official capacity.

But what was that official capacity, he couldn't help thinking as he jumped off the boat in the harbor and waved his thanks to the captain? As he moved through passport control, he watched the surprise on the officials' faces as they recognized him. He cut short their stammered responses. They quickly waved him through until he was out on the streets of Jazira, walking toward the palace, alone for the first time in a long time.

He was still king and should have waited. It wouldn't be long before the formalities were complete, and the hushed-up confidential abdication plans were actioned, but he couldn't wait any longer. Not since he heard the news about the reef.

He knew what she'd thought when she'd approved its joint ownership. He knew what she'd remembered as she'd signed the papers, and he knew what she'd felt because it was the same for him. It was the moment when they'd both realized that what they had was more, much more, than just a one-night stand. The seeds of love had been sown on that day at the beach, and its memory was indelibly written on both their hearts. Her decision showed that her feelings hadn't changed. He remembered her words verbatim. He repeated them often enough to himself.

"The reef is important to both our countries." The press release quoted Shakira. "I've had the best moments of my life swimming close to it." He was probably the only person in the world who knew that the only time she'd swum close to it was with him.

It was enough for him to continue with his plan. He'd put everything in place. He had a question to ask her, a question he hoped she'd answer in the affirmative, now that there were no longer any impediments. Or at least he hoped there weren't. He couldn't be sure of her response, but he was certain that he had to ask her the question. If he didn't, he'd never know what her answer might have been, and he'd have to live with that uncertainty for the rest of his life.

He knew where she went at that hour. She was a leader of her people, and she always went to the early morning market to see and hear her people. It must have been a nightmare for her security, but she got her way—an example of the power she now held.

He watched her as she moved around the market and admired her. He'd wait for her.

BY THE TIME Shakira arrived back at the palace, she was buoyed by the love of her people and smiling. But the smile dropped when she saw who was waiting for her.

"Roshan." His name slipped from her lips. He smiled. It turned out he wasn't a figment of her imagination.

"Shakira," he said, with equal softness.

"But..." She could feel a hot flush suffuse her cheeks which had nothing to do with the heat of the day.

She turned to her advisor, who shook his head in confusion.

"You were not expected, Your Majesty."

He stepped forward. "This is not an official visit, Your Highness. I had hoped for an interview alone with you if that is possible."

The heat turned up a notch as her heart pounded. "Anything is possible. But is it wise? That is another issue altogether."

She was aware of people gathering around her, puzzled as to why she'd stopped, and the identity of the stranger she was talking to. "I... must continue. I can't..." She trailed off, unwilling to admit exactly what she couldn't do.

"You can do anything you like, Your Majesty," smiled Roshan. "I seek only a brief audience, and then if you wish me to leave, I will leave. I am at your command."

"Your Majesty," said one of her guards, after speaking to the microphone on his sleeve. "We are expected at the palace for the morning meeting."

She glanced at the guard, irritated by the pressure. "Tell them..." She looked again at Roshan, and all confusion disappeared. There was no way she could say no to a meeting with him. She fitted together with him like two puzzle pieces forming a whole—yin and yang; positive and negative; male and female. Without taking her gaze from Roshan, she spoke to the guard. "Tell them to delay it for half an hour. Something... has come up."

A look like relief rolled off Roshan, and she realized for the first time that he'd been uncertain as to his reception. It puzzled her. Surely he knew?

"Please," she said as she entered the palace, "come this

way." She turned to her guards. "You may leave us." She ignored their looks of concern and curiosity as they looked at Roshan.

Roshan fell into step beside her and opened the door for her. "I'm not sure your guards think this is a good idea."

"They're not the only ones," she said, on a quickly exhaled breath, and walked through into the private corridor.

"That's because you have a number of wrong ideas about me, Your Majesty. Ideas I intend to put right."

She paused at the entrance to one of the gardens and looked up at him. "Do you now? You must know, Roshan, that I'm not the same woman you knew all those months ago. Circumstances have changed. I've changed."

"I know that. I can see that, and I'm glad. You've grown into the woman you should always have been, in control of your destiny."

She nodded. "And you do not intend to change that?"

"Never. That's the opposite of what I want."

"All right." She indicated the path straight ahead to the pergola by a fountain. "We can talk undisturbed here."

They sat down, and he looked around. "You've been busy. I've seen photos of this place, and it was a mess, partly destroyed."

"Yes. For years, it was derelict after the civil war my country experienced during my grandfather's reign."

"But now you've put it right."

She ran her hand along its new marble base. "It's a symbol of my country, and my feelings for my country. Made anew. With a future."

"You've done well, Shakira."

She turned her head to look at him. It was the first time he'd used her first name. "I'd almost forgotten what my name sounded like. No one calls me that."

"It can be a lonely job, can't it?"

She swallowed and nodded. "It's my duty and my destiny."

"I know," he said quietly. And she was yet again surprised. She'd imagined he'd come to argue with her, to persuade her to do one thing or another.

"Why are you here?" she asked quietly.

He gave a sad smile. "You imagine I'm here to insist that you leave your country and come away with me?"

She bit her lip and nodded. There was no point in arguing. It was exactly what she imagined.

"I'm not, Shakira. Quite the contrary."

She narrowed her eyes, unable to make sense of his meaning.

"I have a proposition for you." Her heart shouldn't have quickened. She thought she had herself under better control than that. It seemed not.

She licked her lips. "A proposition," she repeated faintly. She gave him a quick, uncertain smile. "Business or pleasure?"

He smiled back. "Hopefully both."

"That sounds… complicated." It was the only word for the confusion of feelings and thoughts which his words had engendered.

"On the contrary. It's straightforward." His hand tapped his pocket. Then he withdrew a box and before she knew it, he was on bended knee before her. He opened the box in which lay the largest diamond ring she'd ever seen, sparkling on a bed of deep blue velvet. "Will you marry me, Shakira?"

Her smile dropped. "You know I can't." She jumped up and waved the ring away. "Why go to all this trouble simply to ask me the impossible?"

"Shakira!" He tried to reach for her arm, but she shook it off and stalked over to the far side of the garden.

"Leave me alone, Roshan!" she said, her voice shaking, threatening to undo the tight control with which she'd managed everything over these past few months. "Just leave me alone. You put everything at risk."

But he didn't leave her alone. He came and stood in front of her and gently lifted her chin to force her to look at him. "I threaten to break down that hard exterior you've been forced to create to protect yourself."

"Exactly. How could you, when you know what my answer must be?" Tears threatened. "I need that protection."

"No you don't. You only need it if you're trying to keep something—or someone—out. You only need it to keep your heart from feeling. Do you want to know how I know? Because that's exactly what I've been doing for years. But not anymore. You've made me see that. You've made my heart beat again for something other than making the blood move around my body. You've made it live again and love again. Shakira, I told you I had a proposition, and I do. My brother will shortly take my place as king, sheikh, and leader of Sharq Havilah."

She gasped. Of all the things he could have said, she hadn't imagined this. "No!"

"Yes."

"But you can't! Your country is everything to you."

"Once it was, but no longer. *You* are everything to me. Without you, I have nothing to give anyone else or any country. I'm a shell of a person without you. I need you, Shakira. Will you have me?"

"You're truly giving up your kingdom?"

He nodded.

"But what will you do?"

"That depends. If you agree to marry you, I'll move here and be with you."

"You want to be King of Jazira?" She frowned, quickly assessing the implications. "It can't happen, Roshan. If you become king, my people will be suspicious. They'll imagine you, and the other kings, are trying to take over Jazira."

"I don't want to be king. I don't wish for any power whatsoever in Jazira. And we can formalize that, however you like. I wish to be with you, I wish to support you, and I wish to give you many babies to ensure our family's succession." He put his arms around her and held her tight. "Think about it, Shakira. It will cement our region's security. Our children will be its future."

She shook her head, her frown deepening. "But people will be suspicious. How can they believe you don't wish to take Jazira over?"

"By what you say, by what I say. By my title, or lack of it and by my actions. I'm serious, Shakira. I want nothing from your country, except you. And I'll make it my life's work to show you and your people that that is all I want."

"But your country was everything to you."

"Maybe once. But no longer. *You* are. I cannot have both, so I choose you."

She smiled as relief rolled off her in waves. "I thought I'd changed over the time since we first met, but you've changed more."

"For the better, I hope?" he said, stealing a kiss from her lips.

She swept her finger over his lips and remembered the countless times she'd relived his caresses at night when she'd become tangled in the hot sheets wanting him so much.

"Is this happening to me?" she asked in awe.

"It is if you answer my question."

She grinned. "Remind me what it is again?"

He narrowed his eyes sexily and gave a small grunt. "I suppose you want me on my knees again."

"I do. But not here. Maybe later, in the bedroom." The thought of him in that position and what he would do to her, had her wet with desire. "For now, your Queen requests you to remain standing where she may kiss you if the mood takes her."

"Okay," he said slowly.

"So, where were we? Yes, your question, please."

His hands slid around to the small of her back, and he pulled her tight against him. Their hips were pressed up close; there was only a whisper of air between their lips. "Shakira, my love, will you marry me? Will you take me to your bed, your heart, your mind, your world and live your life with me?"

She licked her lips at the thought of what lay ahead of her. Not just now, but tomorrow, next week, next year, the rest of their lives. An endless time of loving. She nodded. "I will."

Then she curled her hands around his neck and

brought his mouth to hers and kissed him hard and firmly, precisely like a queen should kiss her forbidden lover.

188

EPILOGUE

Shakira sat down thankfully, accepted a glass of lime sharbat, and sighed heavily with relief. It was over. Thank goodness it had gone so well.

Roshan had known it would, and while she'd never voiced her doubts that her people would give him their total support, she couldn't help wondering if they would. Like echoes from a distant past, the doubts had clung to her thoughts, insubstantial but unnerving. And it seems she wasn't the only one who'd had doubts.

"Your new countrymen showed their approval of you, today, Roshan," said Zavian.

"You sound surprised."

Zavian shrugged. "More like astonished."

Amir laughed. "You and me, both."

Their doubts didn't faze Roshan. "I seem to be the only person who didn't doubt our people's feelings toward me."

"And why is that?" asked Amir.

Shakira twisted in her seat to look at the three men talking by the side of the pool. "Because Roshan has worked tirelessly to make it so. He's always out with the people, talking, working, listening." She caught Roshan's loving gaze. "He's my eyes and ears. He knows more about our people than I do."

Roshan rose and took her hand and kissed it. "Only at the moment while you are with child and so tired. After our son is born, we will work together." He kissed her hand again, both his hands now enfolding hers tightly as if he didn't want ever to let her go.

"Side by side," she said, smiling, feeling the heat of his love warming her deep inside. She didn't know where she'd have been these past months without Roshan supporting and guiding her. It seemed running a country was more onerous than she'd imagined, and she would have been lost without his advice, not to mention his love. She sighed, but it was cut short by the baby's foot kicking her in the stomach. She grabbed Roshan's hand and placed it on her swollen belly. He grinned as he felt the movement.

"It has to be a boy," said Ruby, Amir's wife, walking over to them. "Hani was just the same. Constantly wriggling inside of me. Totally unlike Jade who worried the heck out of me. But," she said, pointing to the sleeping baby, "she's just the same peaceful, sleepy baby outside the womb."

"Roshan is adamant that it's a boy, too. Although we don't know for sure. I'd rather it was a surprise. Talking of babies, how's Gabrielle, Zavian?"

"She's very well, thank you. Reluctant to leave the

twins while they're still so young, that's all. She insists on feeding them herself, much to the horror of our staff." Zavian put down his glass. "I must go now, I said I wouldn't be late."

As Zavian left, Xander, Roshan's brother, entered the private courtyard, hands in pockets but with a glower on his face, which only intensified his good looks. Shakira saw the source of the glower a few seconds later as Elaheh's petite figure emerged walking alongside him. Shakira could only hear a general murmur of words coming from Elaheh, and none from Xander. Whatever Elaheh was saying, it didn't look like Xander was impressed.

"Uh-oh," said Roshan. "I'd best go and break those two up."

Shakira frowned. The hostility which had been evident from the day Xander and Elaheh had met concerned her. They were the only source of disagreement amongst the six of them, and it endangered them all.

"Ask Elaheh if she'd come over, would you?" she asked Roshan, who instantly understood.

"Leave it to me," he said. Shakira had the pleasure of watching her husband walk across the garden, enjoying the confident way he walked, his tall, lithe figure and, not least, his behind. She sucked in a breath to control her libido. It was the most distracting thing she had to deal with since becoming queen.

But her attention was broken by Elaheh who walked over to her, her lips pursed and her eyes blazing. She sat next to Shakira with a precise, controlled movement which scarcely betrayed the fire in her eyes.

Shakira sighed. "What's Xander said now?" She didn't have to stand on ceremony with Elaheh. Ever since they'd met, their sisterly bond had grown.

"It's not what he said, it's what he didn't say. Your brother-in-law is maddening! He seems to take pleasure in winding me up and then watching me rant at him."

Shakira shrugged, unable to contradict Elaheh. Xander did, indeed, seem to derive pleasure from teasing Elaheh.

"I'll ask Roshan to have a word with him. We all need to get along to make this peace treaty work."

"I'll not let an arrogant, womanizing son-of-a-bitch—who thinks no woman can take her eyes off him…"

Shakira let her sunglasses drop down onto her nose so she could see Elaheh better. Elaheh hadn't taken her fiery gaze off Xander since she'd come over.

"*You* can't seem to take your eyes off him," she said mildly.

Only then did Elaheh swivel away and look at Shakira with alarm in her eyes. "What?" She shook her head, too vehemently. "Shakira! How can you say such a thing, when it's patently untrue? I cannot bear the man. He's… he's…"

"Handsome? Charming? Intelligent? Witty?"

Elaheh's gaze slid back to the man in question, and she opened her mouth to reply, but no response emerge.

Shakira watched with interest. "A shadow of his brother, it's true, but then I'm biased." She exchanged a grin with Roshan, who had managed to wipe the scowl from Xander's face. She turned back to Elaheh, whose gaze was still fixed on Xander.

"You're staring at him again."

Elaheh blushed beetroot, and Shakira sat up with

surprise as she realized that her observation had hit a raw spot. Her heart sank.

Shakira placed her hand on the kicking heel of her daughter—because she felt, unlike everyone else, that it would be a girl: a feisty, outdoorsy, swimming and soccer-booted kind of girl—and let out a deep sigh.

Oh dear. And there was she, imagining a future of plain sailing; a future of prosperity and peaceful harmony between all their countries. But she hadn't factored Elaheh and Xander into the equation. A queen and a king, both fiery and both wanting the same things—a submissive spouse they could control.

Things were about to become complicated again.

THE END

Buy the next book in the series now!

Surrender to the Sheikh — Playboy sheikh, Xander, wants a

trophy wife, and Elaheh, a fiery sheikha, has no interest in marriage whatsoever.

Here's a review of *Surrender to the Sheikh* to give you a taste of what to expect.

"Gripping from start to finish… I loved the whole series." (Review, Amazon.com)

AFTERWORD

Thank you for reading *The Sheikh's Forbidden Lover*. I hope you enjoyed it! **The Sheikhs of Havilah** series is comprised of:

The Sheikh's Secret Baby
Bought by the Sheikh
The Sheikh's Forbidden Lover
Surrender to the Sheikh (excerpt follows)
Taken for the Sheikh's Harem

You can check out all my books on the following pages. And, if you'd like an email letting you know when my latest release has been published, you can sign up to my email list via my website—dianafraser.com.

Happy reading!

Diana

SURRENDER TO THE SHEIKH

BOOK 4 OF SHEIKHS OF HAVILAH

Playboy sheikh, Xander, wants a trophy wife, and Elaheh, a fiery sheikha, is on the hunt for a submissive husband.

Xander and Elaheh dislike each other at first meeting, and sparks continue to fly as they work with the other Kings of Havilah to bring peace and prosperity to their region.

But the distance they agree to keep from each other is destroyed when Elaheh is forced to accept Xander's protection. Will this forced proximity bring them closer, or set them, and their countries, on a collision course?

Excerpt

"It's getting worse," said Shakira, watching Elaheh, Queen of Tawazun, walk out of the room with a haughty swish of the traditional robes she always wore. "It cannot go on like this."

The cause of Elaheh's abrupt departure—Xander, the newly appointed King of Sharq Havilah—appeared not in the least perturbed. He stood out of earshot on the terrace, hands thrust into his pockets, his habitual frown framing his handsome face.

Roshan also looked concerned as he finished his coffee and pushed away the empty cup. "They need to learn to work together."

"Just staying in the same room together would be a start!" said Amir, with a shake of the head.

"I agree with Shakira," said Zavian. "This can't be allowed to continue. Their enmity could undermine everything we are working towards, the peace we've worked so hard to create."

"They need to learn to work together," said Roshan, thoughtfully, his joined fists tapping against his lips as he surveyed his brother, chatting to one of the blushing maids. "My brother is not accustomed to being conciliatory."

"And nor is Elaheh," murmured Shakira.

Zavian thumped the table lightly. "Then they should work together on the Havilah-Tawazun infrastructure project. Just the two of them. It is a subject dear to both their hearts—"

"If they have hearts," muttered Amir.

"And so they will have to learn to work together in order for the project to succeed." Zavian turned to Roshan.

"What do you think, Roshan? Will your brother be able to work with Elaheh?"

Roshan bit his lip and Shakira could see that he was conflicted. He loved his brother but was concerned at Xander's controlling nature and apparent inability to compromise. He also felt guilty for having abdicated in order to marry her, leaving Xander king of the country he loved dearly. "He'll have to. I'll talk to him."

Shakira squeezed Roshan's hand and shot him a warm supportive smile. "And I'll talk to Elaheh," she said. She turned to Zavian and Amir. "Leave it with us, we'll make them see they have to work together, for all our sakes."

Zavian and Amir exchanged relieved glances.

"Thank you," said Amir. "There's no alternative. They *must* work together or else everything is compromised." He sighed. "They're both fine people… *separately*. It's when they're together that's the problem." He shrugged.

"Trouble is, they're opposites," added Zavian.

As the three men went to join Xander, Shakira remained seated, her hand on her swollen belly. She heard Queen Elaheh's helicopter take off. Her heart sank.

The meeting had been a near disaster. Whenever Xander had spoken, Elaheh had visibly bristled and had given a cutting reply which Xander had ignored. It was like watching some kind of reality TV show—with all the danger and sparkiness and none of the humor. It chilled her to the core. She'd witnessed enough conflict and dissension in her life to know what harm it could do. She just hoped that Zavian's plan would work, despite the fact he'd got the heart of the problem wrong.

"Trouble is," murmured Shakira to herself, "Xander and Elaheh aren't opposites—they're too much alike."

ABOUT THE AUTHOR

I write romances with stories which make you turn the pages, and characters who feel real—whether they be sheikhs, billionaires, knights or everyday people whose lives are usually far from everyday (at least in my books).

A little about me...I'm an avid people watcher, hopeless romantic and dreamer who spends far too much time gazing out the window, imagining scenes where people struggle with life and emotions but always end up happily. Because, yes, I'm also an eternal optimist!

I live in beautiful New Zealand, just north of Wellington in a small village by the sea. It's here, in a sunny window seat overlooking the hills and trees, that I write my books.

Wherever you are in the world, welcome to my little corner, creating worlds where people struggle with life and emotions but are always rewarded with love and happiness in the end. Because that's non negotiable!

I hope you enjoy my books.

Diana

ALSO BY DIANA FRASER

—British Billionaires—

The Billionaire's Contract Marriage

The Billionaire's Impossible CEO

The Billionaire's Secret Baby

British Billionaire Boxed Set (complete series)

—The Sheikhs' Convenient Brides—

Stranded with the Sheikh

Seduced by the Sheikh

—Diamond Sheikhs—

At the Sheikh's Command

At the Sheikh's Bidding

At the Sheikh's Pleasure

Diamond Sheikhs Boxed Set (complete series)

—Secrets of the Sheikhs—

The Sheikh's Revenge by Seduction

The Sheikh's Secret Love Child

The Sheikh's Marriage Trap

Secrets of the Sheikhs Boxed Set (complete series)

—The Sheikhs of Havilah—

The Sheikh's Secret Baby

Bought by the Sheikh

The Sheikh's Forbidden Lover

Surrender to the Sheikh

Taken for the Sheikh's Harem

The Sheikhs of Havilah Boxed Set (complete series)

—Desert Kings—

Wanted: A Wife for the Sheikh

The Sheikh's Bargain Bride

The Sheikh's Lost Lover

Awakened by the Sheikh

Claimed by the Sheikh

Wanted: A Baby by the Sheikh

Desert Kings Boxed Set (1-3)

Desert Kings Boxed Set (4-6)

Desert Kings Boxed Set (complete series)

—Italian Romance—

The Italian's Perfect Lover

Seduced by the Italian

The Passionate Italian

An Accidental Christmas

Italian Romance Boxed Set (complete series)

Awakening his Lady

Norfolk Knights Boxed Set (1-3)

Defending his Lady

Honoring his Lady